"Rick, wou
to my s

"Ever since his dad died, he's been struggling.
I can'

Rick's
moth

"Plea

"I do
Cassie
help Noah," Rick said. "The offer is open to
you, too, if you want."

She shut down—there was no other way to
express it. "Thank you, but I don't talk about
the past. I appreciate whatever you can do for
Noah though."

It was a warning. *Back off.* And yet Rick knew
he was going to have a hard time doing that.
Her husband's death had affected her whether
she admitted it or not.

Don't get involved, his brain chided again.

She's hurting, his soul answered. *Am I not here
to help others? How else can I make amends for my
past?*

He lifted his head and found a pair of beautiful
brown eyes watching him.

Staying focused on his goal definitely wasn't
going to be easy.

Books by Lois Richer

Love Inspired

This Child of Mine
*Mother's Day Miracle
*His Answered Prayer
*Blessed Baby
†Blessings
†Heaven's Kiss
†A Time to Remember
Past Secrets, Present Love
††His Winter Rose
††Apple Blossom Bride
††Spring Flowers,
  Summer Love
§Healing Tides
§Heart's Haven
§A Cowboy's Honor
§§Rocky Mountain Legacy
§§Twice Upon a Time
§§A Ring and a Promise
Easter Promises
"Desert Rose"
‡The Holiday Nanny

‡A Baby by Easter
‡A Family for Summer
‡‡A Doctor's Vow
‡‡Yuletide Proposal
‡‡Perfectly Matched
+North Country Hero
+North Country Family

Love Inspired Suspense

A Time to Protect
**Secrets of the Rose
**Silent Enemy
**Identity: Undercover

*If Wishes Were Weddings
†Blessings in Disguise
**Finders Inc.
††Serenity Bay
§Pennies from Heaven
§§Weddings by Woodwards
‡Love for All Seasons
‡‡Healing Hearts
+Northern Lights

LOIS RICHER

began her travels the day she read her first book and realized that fiction provided an extraordinary adventure. Creating that adventure for others became her obsession. With millions of books in print, Lois continues to enjoy creating stories of joy and hope. She and her husband love to travel, which makes it easy to find the perfect setting for her next story. Lois would love to hear from you via www.loisricher.com, loisricher@yahoo.com or on Facebook.

North Country Family
Lois Richer

HARLEQUIN® LOVE INSPIRED®

Recycling programs for this product may not exist in your area.

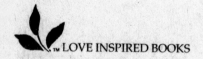

LOVE INSPIRED BOOKS

ISBN-13: 978-0-373-81751-1

NORTH COUNTRY FAMILY

www.Harlequin.com

Printed in U.S.A.

Trust in the Lord with all your heart and lean not to your own understanding. In all your ways acknowledge Him and He will direct your paths.
—*Proverbs* 3:5–6

This book is dedicated to my sister Darcy,
who sees a need, and quietly, in her own way, fills it.

Bless you, Darc.

Chapter One

"My dad's d-dead."

Rick Salinger ignored the December snow-scape outside to study the face of the stuttering boy slouched on the train seat next to him. They'd been talking for the past half hour.

His heart ached for both Noah and his father, but at the moment he felt most saddened by the knowledge that Noah's father would never get to see his son grow and change. That sadness came from the knowledge that Rick would never get to see a son grow and change, either. He would never have a family. Because he didn't deserve one.

"My d-dad stole f-from our ch-church." Noah rubbed one eye then put his glasses back in place. "Th-then he k-killed himself. M-mom said he was t-too a-ashamed to t-tell us."

Rick wanted to hug the kid, but Noah's rigid expression said he wouldn't tolerate that.

"My f-father died r-running away. And now that's wh-what we're d-doing, too."

"Running away?" Rick stared at him, surprised by the disgust in the boy's voice.

"My m-mom calls it s-starting over," Noah muttered.

"That's way different than running away." Rick frowned when the boy shrugged. He tried a different approach. "You and your mom must miss your dad, Noah."

"M-my Mom m-maybe. She c-cries when she th-thinks I c-can't hear her, but I d-don't cry for him." Noah's fingers tightened around his iPod.

"I'm really sorry," Rick told him sincerely. He suppressed a groan. What an inane remark. "That's not much help, is it? But you can pray about it."

"I don't p-pray," Noah said, an edge tingeing his voice. "N-not anymore."

"That's too bad because God hears the prayers of His kids," Rick said softly.

"Maybe He h-hears but He d-doesn't answer." Noah turned his head away.

"God always answers, Noah." A yearning to help this angry, fatherless boy swelled deep inside Rick. "You know, a lot of us make mistakes that we wish we could undo. But that doesn't mean God doesn't hear our prayers."

"Then wh-why doesn't He m-make things d-different?" Noah demanded.

Rick had asked himself that same question a thousand times, mostly whenever he was reminded of his last days as a stockbroker, right after he'd made that last, greedy, too-speculative gamble and lost his clients' money. Seniors, single parents, a fund to help the needy—they'd all put their trust in wonder broker Rick Salinger. And because he was so desperate to prove he was better than the no-account street kid he'd been, he'd skipped the due diligence and invested in a scheme that cost them everything.

With that memory came waves of guilt. For a moment he got sucked into it. Then he shook it off, forcing himself to focus on Noah.

"You want God to wave a magic wand and make it all better?" When Noah nodded, Rick smiled. "That would be nice, but I think God wants us to learn from our mistakes."

Noah didn't look convinced. "How do you kn-know for sure?"

"Because God is a loving Father who wants the best for His kids." Rick stifled a laugh at the look on Noah's face. Clearly the kid had no love for members of the clergy.

"My g-grandfather is a minister, t-too," he said after a long silence.

Rick waited for more information but Noah just added, "I wish m-my mom would w-wake up. I'm s-starving."

As if in answer, an anxious voice across the aisle, two rows back, called, "Noah?"

Rick watched Noah's shoulders tense. He waited for the boy to answer. When he didn't, Rick said,

"He's here. With me." He half rose to identify himself and immediately got caught in the worry-filled stare of the loveliest brown eyes he'd ever seen.

A woman who looked too young to be the mother of this boy stood. She passed a hand over her jeans, straightened a sweater that accentuated the golden glints in her eyes then stepped into the aisle. Her blond hair caressed her cheeks in tumbled layers of tousled curls as she raked a hand through them.

He knew that face.

Rick scrambled to remember where he'd seen her before but came up blank. He was positive that he knew her, though Noah's mother didn't seem to know him. She barely glanced at him before she hunkered down beside her son.

"You were supposed to tell me if you were going somewhere, Noah."

Rick immediately understood that the harshness he heard in her voice came from the fear still lingering in her eyes. A mental image of her— younger, without the worry, carefree and happy— flashed through his head.

Where did that come from?

"S-sorry, Mom," Noah muttered. He didn't sound sorry.

"Noah didn't want to wake you so he moved over here. We've been chatting to pass the time." He thrust out a hand. "I'm Rick Salinger."

Instantly a barrier went up in her cocoa-toned eyes. After several moments' hesitation she slid her small hand into his for about half a second then immediately pulled it away.

"Cassie Crockett," she said with her chin thrust forward. "I'm sorry Noah bothered you."

"He didn't— Just the opposite, actually. Did you know your son is a cardshark?" Rick was certain he'd never met anyone named Cassie Crockett so he couldn't possibly know her, and yet that face...

Rick regrouped and grinned at Noah. "He beat me in six straight games of hearts."

"I've been there." A smile flickered at the corner of her lips. "Humbling, isn't it?"

"Very," Rick agreed, wanting to see what a real smile looked like on Cassie Crockett. "But I was glad to have someone to talk to. Seventeen hours from Thompson to Churchill makes for a long ride, even if this part of northern Canada is the best of God's creation." He paused then asked, "Have we met before?"

"No." Short and succinct, her answer flew out almost before he'd finished asking the question.

"I don't mean to push it, but you seem very familiar to me," he said.

"I assure you, I have never seen you before." She held his gaze, dark brown sparks in her eyes defiant.

"I'm h-hungry, Mom." Noah looked at Rick, and seemed to sense an ally. "I b-bet Pastor Rick is hungry, t-too. We want b-breakfast."

"Pastor?" Cassie's voice squeaked. Her heart-shaped face paled as her eyes narrowed.

"H-he's a minister in C-Churchill." Noah seemed either unaware of or unconcerned about his mother's reaction.

"I am." Rick sensed that a change of subject would be helpful. "They serve a passable breakfast on board, Mrs. Crockett." He smiled again, hoping to allay whatever fears made her tense. "I could show you the way."

"That's okay," she said, her voice colder than before. "We're not ready yet."

"I'm r-ready, Mom," Noah contradicted.

"We have to clean up first." Cassie's brow furrowed as she studied her son. "Your hair needs combing."

"Then c-can we have breakfast with P-Pastor Rick?"

Noah's blue eyes begged her, but Cassie seemed to be searching for an excuse not to join him, so Rick gave her an out.

"Maybe I'll see you there." He grinned at Noah. "It was nice meeting you. Thanks for the card game."

"It was n-nice m-meeting you, too," Noah responded. "T-thanks for telling m-me about Churchill. If we g-go to a r-restaurant, I'm g-going to order c-c-caribou."

"Good. But if anyone offers you *muktuk,* make sure it's fresh." Rick hid his smile and waited for the inevitable question.

"Wh-why?"

"Whale skin and blubber are best eaten fresh."

Rick chuckled at Noah's dismayed look. "It's actually not bad when you get used to it." Then he nodded at Cassie. "Excuse me."

Apparently Cassie hadn't realized she was blocking his way. Her cheeks flamed bright pink as she stepped out of the way and beckoned to Noah to follow.

Rick tried not to hear their discussion as he waited for another passenger to move out of the aisle, but it was difficult not to eavesdrop.

"Why d-didn't we go with Pastor R-rick, Mom? I'm s-starving." Noah's stutter seemed to worsen with his temper. "I w-want to g-go n-now."

"Noah, behave." Cassie sounded irritated. "We'll go for breakfast soon, but not if you're going to make a fuss. That is not how a Crockett behaves," she said softly, almost too softly for Rick to hear.

"Mrs. P-Perkins said all C-crocketts behave b-badly," Noah muttered in a sullen tone.

"Mrs. Perkins was wrong." Cassie sounded desperate to shush her son.

"Th-that's what she said about y-you," Noah retorted. "Sh-she said you m-made the b-b-biggest mistake of your l-life."

Able to finally move forward to the dining car, Rick couldn't hear Cassie's response. Noah's words had raised a thousand questions in his mind—but first and foremost was this: Why, when she'd learned his profession, had she shrunk away from him as if he had the plague?

That question was quickly followed by another: Why did her offended look bother him so much?

In the dining car, Ned Blenkins stood waiting to take his order.

"Nice to see you again, Preacher. Same as usual?" Ned asked with his cheery smile.

"Yes, please." Rick accepted a cup of coffee.

"Won't take a minute," Ned promised.

Rick carried his steaming cup to the only empty table. Though most of the other passengers had finished their meals and now lingered over coffee, no one invited him to join them. He took a seat, reminding himself that eating alone didn't bother him. He deserved a lot worse than a solitary breakfast, he thought with a pang of fresh guilt.

Rick had seen most of the other people in the dining car around Churchill, though not in his church. He knew each member of his small congregation personally, and he suspected they all knew about his ugly past. In a small town like Churchill there were few secrets.

He'd been very honest in telling the hiring committee how he'd lost every dime of his own and that of every client who'd trusted him. He'd also told them how he'd found God, and of his vow to serve Him in an effort to rectify the wrongs he'd done. Though none of his parishioners had ever confronted him about it, Rick figured it was the reason why he hadn't attracted any new parishioners. Who wanted to attend the church of a man who'd caused such harm?

As he waited for his breakfast, Rick glanced at the paper his neighbor was reading. His heart took a nosedive when he saw the headline of a small piece in the bottom right corner—"Local couple loses bid to sue publisher for risky book on investing."

"Not again," his soul cried.

He grabbed the paper off his own table and read the entire section. The leaden weight in his stomach grew as he read about a young couple desperate to have children. They needed money for fertility procedures. Now they were homeless because they'd mortgaged their house and sold everything they owned to invest their money after they'd read a book called *Untold Riches in the Stock Market.* Rick had written the book under the same pseudonym the publisher had used for six other how-to books in the same series. It was doubtful his authorship would ever be made public because Rick had signed a confidentiality agreement. But that didn't ease any of his guilt.

Almost five years later and there were still ramifications. Worse, he was powerless to stop it.

He read that the court ruled that though the book offered risky—perhaps even foolhardy—advice, the advice was not illegal and the lawsuit had been dismissed.

Oh Lord, he prayed silently. *How can I ever atone for all the pain my greed has caused?*

Overwhelmed by guilt, Rick had promised God that last day at the seminary that he'd give up his most precious dream—he'd clung to it all through the years he'd scrabbled to stay alive on the streets of Toronto—the dream of having a home and a family. Those two things were all he'd ever wanted—a place to call his own, and people who loved and cared for him.

It had cost Rick dearly to sacrifice that dream, but every time he learned of someone else who'd suffered because of him, he renewed his vow. It was his way of showing God he was worthy of His love.

But was he?

Defeat nagged at Rick as he thought about the eight months he'd been ministering in Churchill. By most measures, the lack of new members in his church probably meant he was a failure as a minister. But he'd promised God he'd serve where he was placed and for now, that place was Churchill. All he could do was his best until God sent him somewhere else.

"Eggs over easy with bacon." Ned set the loaded plate in front of him.

"Thanks, Ned." Rick palmed him a generous tip.

He'd barely lifted his head from saying grace when the door burst open and Noah stalked in, followed by Cassie. She quickly realized there was no empty table and frowned. Her brown eyes narrowed as she endured curious stares.

"Come and join me," Rick invited, rising. Noah didn't even glance at his mother for permission before he strode over. Cassie followed more slowly.

"We don't want to bother you," she said.

"You're not," he assured her. "You're welcome here."

Cassie hesitated.

"Come on, Mom. I'm s-starving."

Cassie ignored Noah, her gaze locked on Rick. She studied him for what seemed like ages before she inclined her head in an almost imperceptible nod.

"Thank you. We'd like to join you." She laid a hand on Noah's shoulder. "On a scale of one to ten, how hungry are you?"

"F-fourteen." Noah slouched on the chair beside Rick as Cassie turned to place their order. His eyes widened at the sight of Rick's plate. "F-four eggs?"

"I guess I'm an eighteen on your scale." Rick laughed at Noah's surprise but his gaze was already back on Cassie as she made her way toward Ned. He could still smell her fragrance. Whatever it was, it suited her. Soft, very feminine with a hint of spice. Feisty.

You're thinking about this woman entirely too much. Do not get involved.

"W-won't you get f-fat?" the boy asked, his forehead pleated in a frown.

"I hope not." Rick hid his smile. After reading that article he was no longer hungry. He offered Noah the plate with the extra toast he'd ordered. Noah selected one half slice.

"Mrs. P-Perkins said my m-mom is f-fat," he muttered.

"No offense, but I think Mrs. Perkins, whoever she is, must need glasses." Rick smiled. "Your mom is beautiful," he added.

"I g-guess s-so." Silence reigned as Noah devoured his toast.

Cassie returned a few moments later with two glasses of juice and a cup of coffee. She raised one eyebrow at Noah when he reached for a second slice of Rick's toast but said nothing as she set the juice in front of him.

"Th-that's it?" Noah demanded. He looked at Rick sadly. "M-maybe *I'm* f-fat."

When Cassie chuckled, Rick focused on her face. Again he tried to recall where and when he'd seen her before, but, truthfully, it didn't matter. What mattered was that here was a kid who'd lost his dad and a woman who'd lost her husband, and there was something wrong between them. Maybe he could help. Maybe, if he could, he would find a measure of peace.

Churchill was his proving ground. If he couldn't do God's work here—if he couldn't help this community or kids like Noah—what good was he? And if his ministry failed, how could he ever earn forgiveness? Failure in Churchill meant it was doubtful another church would give him a chance.

God, I came here to make amends. Please help me do that for these hurting hearts.

But even if Rick could help this mother and son, he knew he'd never earn redemption.

"They have to cook your breakfast, Noah. It'll be here in a few minutes."

Cassie sat, her brow furrowing as she leaned near Noah's ear. "Please stop repeating things Mrs. Perkins said. I know she was angry. A lot of church members were. But most of what she said isn't true."

"Wh-which part *is* t-true?" Noah asked in a sour tone.

Cassie gave him a chiding look. She sipped her coffee and worked hard to look anywhere but at Rick. That green-eyed stare of his saw too much.

"Are you two visiting Churchill for long?" Rick smiled.

"We're n-not v-visiting." Noah eyed Rick's remaining slice of toast. Rick nodded. "M-my mom's going to work at l-luck."

Noah's struggle to get the word out pierced Cassie's heart. The pain doubled when Noah noticed the other patrons' stares and ducked his head in shame.

"Luck?" Rick shook his head. "I don't think I know it."

"Lives Under Construction—LUC. It's a rehabilitation facility where troubled boys are sent to serve their time in the justice system. We shortened it," Cassie explained.

"Very clever. And I am very familiar with

Lives—that's the shortened form we use here." He smiled at Noah's wide eyes when Ned set a loaded platter in front of him. "Here's your breakfast."

"N-not s-sure if I'm *th-that* hungry, Mom," the boy said.

"I thought we could share, especially since you ate Mr., uh, Pastor—*his* toast." Cassie felt her cheeks heat up. Why did this man fluster her? "I'm sorry but I don't know what to call you."

"Rick will do just fine."

"Rick it is." Cassie accepted an empty plate from Ned with a smile of thanks. She liberated an egg, a slice of toast and one strip of bacon from Noah's plate.

"Mrs. Crockett, are you the nurse Laurel's been expecting?" Rick's green eyes flared with surprise.

"Yes." Cassie added no other information. She figured his surprise now equaled hers, when she'd found out he was a minister. With his short, spiky dark hair, day-old chin stubble and that easy grin that embraced everyone, Rick looked nothing like the ministers she knew. "How did you know?"

"Laurel told me she'd hired someone." Rick must have understood the question on her face because he added, "Laurel Quinn and I are good friends. I go to Lives Under Construction a lot to work with the boys."

"Oh. Then you probably also know she has three clients with special needs arriving. The government insists she have a medical person on the premises to monitor their care." Cassie tasted her bacon and toast before continuing. "I'm also hoping to work a few shifts at the hospital while the boys are in school."

"That shouldn't be an issue. The health center can always use more help and the Inuit Transient Center will welcome you with open arms." Rick's attention slid to Noah who, having cleaned his plate leaned back in his chair. Rick smiled.

"Something about my job amuses you?" Hearing the belligerence in her voice, Cassie wished she'd controlled it. But she'd endured mockery once too often recently from people who claimed to be her friends and then doubted her.

"No, ma'am. Something about him amuses me."

Rick chuckled when Noah drained his juice glass and smacked his lips. "Feel better?"

"Much." Noah grinned.

Cassie's heart brimmed with adoration for this child of hers. Noah, twelve, had suffered deeply and dealt with so much since Eric's death. She'd made this move to Churchill hoping to restore the fun-loving kid he'd been before his father's death and the two years of misery that had followed.

Cassie suddenly noticed Rick studying Noah with an odd look. Was that longing in his forest-green eyes? As she wondered if he had any children of his own, a hundred questions about Rick Salinger suddenly swarmed her.

You can't trust him, she thought. *You trusted Eric and your father and they weren't there for you. Eric never even confided in you about losing*

*those church funds. And then he was too proud to
face his mistakes. You've paid for that a hundred
times over and so has Noah. Now it's time to get
on with your lives. Alone.*

Cassie shut off the painful reminders. "Are there
many churches in Churchill?" she asked.

Rick blinked and the shadows in his eyes dis-
sipated.

"Four at the moment. Mine is the smallest."

"Because?" She chewed on a slice of toast while
she waited for his answer.

"That's hard to say." He frowned. "It's either because I'm not very good at my job or because I'm
not giving the kind of message people want to hear."
He shrugged. "I'll leave it to you to decide, Cassie."

So different than her father. *He* would have insisted it wasn't his fault, that people were too hard-
hearted to hear the truth. She liked that Rick took
responsibility.

"I'm sure folks will come around in time," she
murmured.

"I hope so, but that's God's job." He smiled,
clearly comfortable in his skin. That also made a
positive impression on Cassie. Too many people
were out to impress and didn't care who they hurt
in the process. That's why she'd stopped trusting.

That's why she'd come to Churchill.

"W-will we go to P-Pastor Rick's c-church,
Mom?" Noah asked.

"We'll see." The age-old parental response
her father had always given seemed to fit. When

she glanced up, she found Rick's attention on her again. From the speculative way he studied her, she thought he knew that he wouldn't be seeing them in his pews anytime soon.

"W-we haven't gone to ch-church for a long t-time," Noah mused, staring out the window. His forehead pleated in a frown of distaste as he glanced back at Rick. "My g-grandfather y-yells."

"Some preachers do," Rick agreed in a mild tone.

Cassie liked that Rick didn't prod Noah for more information. In fact, there was a lot about this man that she was beginning to like, and that made her nervous.

"My father is—was—a minister. He's retired now." She winced at her tone. A man like Rick, attuned to people's nuances, would realize she disliked mentioning him.

"I see." Rick grinned at Noah. "Don't worry, Noah. I don't yell in church. I mostly just talk. You're welcome to come anytime." He checked his watch then rose. "Will you excuse me? I've got some reading to do before we arrive."

Noah's blue eyes sparkled. "I c-can hardly w-wait to see Aunt L-Laurel."

"I didn't realize you were related." Rick's curious gaze turned on Cassie.

"Laurel and I met years ago in Toronto when I worked in pediatrics," Cassie explained. "She brought in clients from time to time and we became friends. Noah was very young then. He sort of adopted her. We've kept in touch over the years. I guess that's why she thought of me when she needed help with Lives."

"I'm sure you'll be a great asset, Cassie. We can use all the help we can get to reach Laurel's boys."

Cassie searched Rick's face. *We.* That meant they'd be working together. Would he judge her, too, when he found out about Eric? As she stood, she looked around at the Christmas decorations still hanging in the dining car. "It seems funny that there are only three days till New Year's Eve."

"Churchill's New Year's Eve is fantastic," Rick said.

"Wh-why?" Noah demanded.

"You'll have to go to find out. But I will tell you this—it's a town-wide party with amazing fireworks."

Rick gestured for them to precede him out of the dining car. Cassie felt stares as they walked toward their seats. She automatically smoothed a hand over her hip, then stopped herself. Her jeans were years out of date and her leather boots had seen far better days, but why should she care what Rick or anyone else thought about her?

She took a look around and saw that most of her fellow passengers, including Rick, looked as though they chose function over fashion.

They're not judging you, Cassie.

As she and Noah reached their seats, she glanced back and saw Rick joking with a woman nearby as he pulled a duffel bag from the overhead rack.

He hadn't said anything about a wife or kids and he didn't wear a ring, but Cassie felt certain that a man with Rick's looks wasn't single unless he wanted it that way. He was too charming for it to be otherwise.

And nice, her brain prodded. Rick was definitely nice.

Cassie took a seat and closed her eyes. Pastor Rick Salinger was a mystery all right, but not one Cassie was going to explore. After the mess Eric had left her in and the condemnation of her church family, she just wanted to keep things as simple as possible. She would do her job and build a new life at Lives Under Construction. If she failed to get Noah straightened out here—well, she couldn't fail, that was all. Churchill was her last resort.

An ache tore through Cassie as she studied Noah. Since Eric's death Noah had been acting out. He'd been disciplined at school for his bad behavior and she'd tried to discipline him at home. Neither had worked. He'd progressively become more of an opponent than the son she adored.

She had to get him to change the path he was on, to let go of the brooding anger inside before he did something she couldn't fix.

Her gaze roamed the train until it rested on Rick. Rick said he helped the boys at Lives. Maybe he could—she didn't dare let herself think it.

Cassie Crockett had learned the hard way that you couldn't trust anyone.

It was a lesson she'd never forget.

Chapter Two

The weight of Cassie's decision hit when she opened her eyes an hour later and got her first view of Churchill.

She was alone, a single mom with a troubled kid to support in a cold, barren land where she had just one friend, Laurel. Had moving here been the right decision?

The train jerked. They were slowing down.

It didn't matter now if the decision was right or wrong. It had been made.

"We're here, M-Mom," Noah said. For the first time in many months a hint of excitement colored his voice.

The tired old train ground to a stop with much squeaking of brakes. Noah jumped to his feet. Cassie reached up to heft her overnight case from the storage compartment above. A hand slid over hers where it grasped the suitcase handle.

"Yes, Noah. I'm hurrying—"

The words died away when she turned and stared into Rick's dark green gaze.

"Let me help you with this."

Odd how his quiet offer made her feel as if she wasn't quite so alone.

Cassie nodded, swallowing when his warm fingers eased the handle from her hands, lifted the bag free and shifted it so it would roll forward. "Thank you."

"You're welcome." His low response, for her ears alone, made her feel cared for. She liked that.

You have no business liking anything about Rick, she scolded herself.

But the scolding didn't seem to stop her from appreciating the tall, lean man. A slanted smile played on his too-handsome face, warming her like a ray of sunshine. His easy manner made her drop her guard, feel comfortable. The pull of attraction toward him was like nothing she'd known before. She searched his eyes, trying to understand the connection she felt, ignoring the flutter in her stomach when he met her gaze.

"I appreciate your entertaining Noah during the ride," she said as they waited to disembark.

"He's a great kid." The pastor took her arm to help her as they stepped outside, grinning at Noah's astonished reaction to mountainous snowdrifts that dazzled in the brilliant morning sun. "Welcome to Churchill."

As they moved away from the crowd and down the platform, Rick stayed by her side, matching his strides to her shorter ones, rolling her case along as if it were a feather. He had the long, lean grace of a distance runner. Though Cassie noticed the many admiring stares he received, Rick didn't seem to. He smiled and greeted people, totally at ease.

By contrast, Noah stood aloof, surveying the area with a wariness Cassie wished she could help him shed. But how? Noah argued with her constantly over the least little thing. Nothing Cassie had tried seemed to help reduce the stutter that had appeared several months earlier. Not even prayer.

"Noah could go inside to stay warm," Rick told her. "But it's better if you wait here for the opening of the container car to ensure all your stuff has arrived. If it doesn't, you have to make a claim right away. You do have more than this?" he asked, indicating her suitcase.

"Oh, yes." Cassie nodded. "We have more."

Laurel had explained to Cassie that she should bring as much as she could and take advantage of the railway's free transportation of patrons' goods because shipping in everyday things could make living in the North Country very expensive.

As Cassie looked around at the vast glistening beauty of the isolated land, she decided the expense of living so far north was worth it when she would be able to savor this view every day. Maybe she hadn't made a mistake coming here. Maybe life for her and Noah was finally going to get better.

She shifted from one foot to the other, glad of her coat's thick insulation, as endless pallets of bulky paper items were off-loaded followed by boxes and trunks of all descriptions. As Rick retrieved the items she pointed out, Cassie became conscious of odd looks, the kind that said the onlookers suspected they were a couple. She stepped away from him to create some distance as she counted her containers.

"Everything is here," she said.

"Good. And there are my snowshoes." Rick strode forward and picked up a mesh bag.

"Do you like to snowshoe?" Cassie asked.

"I don't know. I haven't tried yet. I bought these at a thrift store in Thompson." He chuckled at her dubious look. "My friend Kyle—he works at Lives, too—promised to teach me." He swung the bag over his shoulder only to set it down again when his cell phone rang. "Excuse me."

He looked at the caller ID, grinned at Cassie and put the phone on speaker.

"Rick? This is Laurel. I'm sorry to bother you but my van conked out." Though Laurel's frustration carried clearly in the crisp air, Cassie felt a measure of relief at hearing her friend's voice. "I'm at the garage and they say it has to stay overnight."

"But you're supposed to pick up your new nurse and her son," Rick guessed with a wink at Cassie. She couldn't help smiling back. There was something about his irrepressible good humor that drew her in.

"Yes, that's why I'm calling. I wondered if you might be able to give us all a ride back to Lives."

"I can because, fortunately for you, I left the block heater on my car engine plugged in while I was in Thompson," Rick said. "It should start without any trouble."

Cassie tracked his gaze to the thermometer on the side of the depot—minus twenty-eight degrees Celsius. No wonder she was shivering.

"I'll have to walk home to get it, though," Rick continued. "You're still at the garage, right? Why don't you stay put until I can pick you up?"

"I just collected one of the boys. How about if we meet you at the station? But before you leave could you find Cassie Crockett and her son and ask them to wait? She's blond, short curly hair—"

"I've already met her and Noah. In fact, Cassie's standing beside me."

"Hi, Laurel," Cassie called.

"Cassie! I can't wait to see you! We'll be there soon. Thanks, Rick."

"No worries, Laurel. See you in a bit." Rick tucked his phone back in his pocket. "You'd better wait inside until I get back." He blinked at the number of boxes and containers on the dock. "Where's the kitchen sink?" he teased.

"We—um, sold our house so we had to bring most of what was left," she explained.

Rick nodded, seeming to sense her discomfort. He hailed a man and introduced Cassie and Noah. "I was wondering if you'd be willing to use your truck to transport Mrs. Crockett's things to Lives Under Construction, George."

"Happy to, Pastor, but it might take a second trip. Lucy Clow's got me picking up a bunch of stuff she bought online."

"Again? Wonder what deals she found this time." Rick shared a grin of understanding with the other man then told Cassie, "Lucy's infamous for her online purchases, which she always donates to something in town. Will picking up your stuff later work for you, Cassie?"

"Later is perfect." Cassie noted the obvious affection between Rick and the older man. "Thank you, Mr. Stern."

"Cassie's going to be the new nurse at Lives Under Construction, George. She's also hoping for some part-time work at the health center." Rick gave her a small nod, as if to say, *Wait for it.*

"Well isn't that a blessing?" George beamed. "Our health board has been trying to find another nurse for ages. You've got work whenever you want, Miss."

"Thank you very much, Mr. Stern." Breathless at the speed with which she'd found a second job, Cassie turned to Rick as George left. "Thank you for doing that."

"My pleasure." He checked his watch. "My place is about three blocks away. I'll have to let the car warm up so it'll be a while before I return. But Laurel should be here shortly. You and Noah can wait inside." Rick slid his hand under her elbow and steered her into the station. Noah followed without saying anything.

The peremptory way Rick directed her without waiting for her agreement triggered her dislike of being controlled. A host of memories of Eric's constant advice and bossy ways filled her head. Eric had seemed to believe she was unable to think for herself. He'd always tried to steer her, literally, and she'd always hated that.

Cassie jerked her arm free once they were inside the depot. "I could have arranged things for myself," she heard herself saying. "You didn't have to ask a stranger—"

"There aren't any strangers in Churchill, Mrs. Crockett," Rick interrupted in a gentle tone. "Up here we try to help each other because we might be the next in need."

"Of course," she whispered, contrite that she'd allowed her past to cause her to behave rudely. "I apologize. Thank you for everything. And please, Rick, call me Cassie." She forced herself to offer a tiny smile. "Noah and I will wait for you over there." She pointed to a bench in the corner.

Rick's good-natured grin returned. He pulled a pair of knitted gloves from his pocket and put them on. "See you in a bit." Swinging his snowshoes onto his shoulder, Rick picked up his duffel and headed out of the station, toward the street that lay beyond the parking lot, obviously enjoying the brisk air.

Cassie glanced at Noah. Eyes closed, earbuds firmly in place, he swayed back and forth to his music, in his own world. She'd leave him alone, for now, but soon she'd have to find a way to get him to break free of his self-imposed isolation.

Her attention returned to the window and the minister who strode across the white-covered terrain. Rick Salinger unnerved her. Not only because of what he said or did but also because of who he was—a minister, like her father.

That was a very big hurdle in her book.

He's also straightforward, full of life and interesting.

All the same, Cassie was determined to keep her distance. No matter how much Rick piqued her interest.

As Rick sauntered back into the train station more than half an hour later, his brain was still struggling to put together a puzzle called Cassie Crockett. One minute she was standoffish and defensive, the next her barriers dropped away and she was warm and engaging. Was that only with him?

And why did he still feel as if he'd met her before?

Cassie sat in the corner where she'd said she'd be, but this was a totally different woman from the one who'd yanked her arm from his grip. She was laughing at something Laurel said, blond head thrown back, eyes dancing. For the first time since he'd met her, Rick thought she looked truly at ease.

"So you met Rick," he heard Laurel say.

"Yes." Cassie's low voice gave nothing away. Though her eyes widened when she saw him, her glance bounced off him, keeping his presence secret.

"He's a great guy and an even better pastor," Laurel said. Rick listened unabashedly while she spent several moments extolling his virtues. "You'll never make a better friend than Rick."

"Well, thank you, Laurel. I love you, too." Rick grinned when the older woman squealed in surprise, turned and then hugged him, ruffling his hair.

Rick basked in the feeling of being cared for. Since a wife and family were never going to be part of his future, he cherished every friendship God brought into his life.

"It's good to have you back, pal." Laurel patted his shoulder.

"Thanks. Who's this?" he asked, nodding at a boy who, like Noah, sat with earphones in his ears, swaying to music no one else could hear.

"This is Bryan." Laurel nudged the boy's shoulder.

In a desultory fashion, Bryan withdrew one headphone. "Yeah?"

"This is Rick, our pastor," Laurel said.

"Dude." Bryan slowly lifted his hand to shake Rick's. His grip was weak, his palms sweaty. Duty done, he immediately replaced his earphone and closed his eyes.

"I'm overwhelmed by my welcome," Rick joked.

"You got a better reception than I did," Cassie complained.

"If he ignored a beautiful woman like you, I don't feel so bad." Surprised he'd spoken his thoughts aloud, Rick glanced at Laurel. The smug smile on her face bothered him, but Rick ignored it. He leaned nearer Cassie. "We'll have to show him that we demand proper respect," he whispered with a conspiratorial wink. Then he turned to Laurel. "On my way in I noticed George has already picked up Cassie's things from the dock so I'm ready to leave here whenever you are."

Noah and Bryan picked up some of the luggage. Rick took the rest. Somehow everything fit inside his small car. Laurel insisted Cassie take the front seat beside him so she'd have a better view of her new home, but Rick noticed Cassie sat just about as far away from his as she could.

"We're off," he said as he fastened his seat belt. He left the parking lot and turned the corner to the highway, noticing Cassie's tight grip on her armrest when the tires slipped on a patch of ice before the treads caught.

"All this ice—" She made a quick glance over one shoulder at Noah.

"It's okay, Cassie." He smiled to reassure her. "Josephina will get us there safely. She isn't the prettiest vehicle around, but she almost always gets where she's going."

"Josephina?" she said. One perfect eyebrow arched. "Why not Joseph?"

"Joseph was a truck, my last vehicle." Rick made sad face. "He wasn't reliable at all."

"We won't go there, then," she said. The amusement on her face sent an unexpected quiver through him.

His brain instantly shot out warnings, reminding him to avoid entanglements. He was here to atone for his past, not get involved. That thought brought a tiny flicker of sadness that he fought to ignore.

"I promise you'll arrive in one piece," he said, noting her grip hadn't eased.

"But which piece?" Cassie teased in a tight voice. Once they were on the highway, she seemed to relax. "Just before Christmas I was in a fender bender in Toronto on very slick roads. I guess I'm still a bit skittish."

"We'll be there soon," he assured her.

Cassie glanced his way, her head tipped to one side. "Do you ever have doubts about anything, Rick?"

The question made him blink as memories from a host of very bad days from his past made him wince.

"You have no idea," he muttered as guilt rolled in.

Cassie studied him, a tiny frown marring her beauty. After that she remained silent until they reached Lives. Rick didn't mind. Her question had sobered him.

"We're home," he said as he turned off the motor.

"Finally." Bryan quickly unfolded himself from the backseat.

"A tall guy like you, you'll be glad Laurel has a

van." Rick watched him stretch. Something about the kid didn't seem right. When Bryan headed for the house, Rick called him back.

"Your bag?" he reminded.

"What, no bell boys?" Bryan attempted a laugh but it fell short. He swiped a hand across his face to remove a sheen of sweat, which was odd given the frosty temperature.

Rick also noticed that Bryan's hand shook when he reached for the suitcase handle. The boy seemed confused as he struggled to maneuver his way to the door. Several times he veered off the pathway into the snow. Concerned by Bryan's unsteadiness, Rick moved to assist him. He arrived just in time to catch Bryan as he slumped.

"Cassie!" Rick yelled. She was there in a second with Laurel.

"Bryan's just been diagnosed with diabetes," Laurel said.

"Get him inside and lay him on the floor," Cassie ordered after a quick look. "Laurel, we'll need some orange juice or something sweet."

Totally out of his depth, Rick appreciated Cassie's orders. He carried Bryan inside then propped up the boy's head as Cassie dribbled some orange juice in his mouth.

"What's wrong with him?" he asked.

"I'm guessing his blood sugar's too low." Concern darkened Cassie's eyes as she monitored the boy's pulse and checked his pupils. "Bryan, when did you last test?" she asked loudly when his eyelids fluttered.

"Didn't." His head lolled into unconsciousness.

Cassie hissed out a sigh of frustration. She looked at Rick. "Can you go through his suitcase and find a small case? It would have test strips, syringes and a vial in it."

Rick did as she asked. When he found the container, he unzipped it and held it open in his palm so she could easily get what she needed.

"Thanks." With precise movements Cassie pricked Bryan's finger and swiped it over a test strip, which she then stuck into the small monitor. She grimaced at the reading, measured out the correct dose from the vial and injected it into Bryan's stomach. After a quick glance at Noah who stood watching, she offered him a smile then returned to monitoring her patient.

Rick noted the tender hand Cassie swept across Bryan's forehead and the kindhearted words she spoke. To anyone watching, Bryan might have been her own child.

"Why didn't he inject himself?" he asked, keeping his voice hushed.

"The doctor's report says he's struggling to accept his illness." Laurel stood beside Noah, watching.

"A lot of kids do," Cassie explained. "They think that if they ignore it, it will go away." She looked at Rick, grim certainty in her eyes. "It won't go away. Bryan's got to learn to handle his diabetes or it will kill him."

"Then we'll help him do that," Rick assured her.

Cassie gave him a funny look before she turned her attention to Bryan once more.

"Okay, he's coming around. Laurel, could you bring a wet cloth? Can you help him sit, Rick?"

"Sure." He slid his arm around Bryan's back and eased him upright. "Take it easy, big guy." When Bryan's bleary gaze met his, he teased, "Is this any way to begin your first day here? Forgetting to take your medication?"

"I didn't forget," Bryan said, slurring his words a bit, but fully aware.

"You must have forgotten," Rick told him in a serious tone. "Because deliberately not taking it sounds dumb, and I don't think you're dumb." He sounded more confident than he felt, and he prayed that God would use his words to help Bryan. "Diabetes is not a death sentence."

"It feels like one to me." Bryan accepted Rick's hand to pull himself upright. He wavered a bit before plopping on a kitchen chair.

"Diabetes isn't the end of your life, Bryan." Rick sat across from him. "In fact, it could be the start of a new life for you, a new beginning here at Lives Under Construction."

Bryan glanced at Laurel and Cassie as if to ask if Rick was serious. But after a moment his gaze returned to Rick, who caught a flicker of curiosity under the boy's tough attitude.

"New start?" the boy demanded. "How?"

"Well, think about it. Nobody here knows you or what you did before you came here. You've got a chance to begin a new year with a clean slate." One glance at Cassie's serious face told Rick he had to make his words count. "Managing your diabetes can be your first step to making your future into whatever you want."

"You make it sound easy," Bryan muttered.

"Oh, no, I didn't say that. But nobody but you can decide your future, Bryan." Rick paused to let that sink in. "You have to choose if you'll waste the opportunity you've been given at a new life, or accept the challenge and use this time to figure out how to build yourself a better world."

Bryan snorted. "I never heard anyone claim going to juvie was getting a break."

"Well, then, let me be the first to offer you a new perspective. Besides, this is not juvenile detention. It's where lives are under construction, on the way to being changed." Rick held his breath, waiting for the boy to decide.

Bryan studied him for a long time, his eyes searching. Rick could tell that he was at least thinking about what he'd heard.

"You should rest for a while, Bryan," Cassie said.

"Yeah. I feel tired. The plane was bumpy. The guy guarding me got sick." He pushed to his feet and followed Laurel to the room he'd been assigned.

Rick rubbed a hand across his face, silently praising God for His help.

"How did you know to do that?"

Rick blinked. Cassie stood in front of him, a puzzled expression on her face. "Do what?"

"Talk to him like that, get him to face his issues and see them from a new perspective." She frowned. "You convinced Bryan he could start over. I think maybe you got through to him. How?"

Shifting under her intense stare, Rick knew there was more to her question than simple curiosity. He glanced around, saw Noah seated in a corner with the luggage, earbuds back in place.

"I prayed for the right words, Cassie. If they hit home it was because God used them, as He used you," he added.

"Me?" she said, almost rearing back in surprise.

"You treated Bryan as if he were Noah," he said softly. "You cared for him with love and tenderness. He felt that. All I did was try to help him see that not everything in his life is bad. There is good in the world if he'll only drop his defenses and accept it."

"But the words you used—" Her voice trailed away.

"Lives Under Construction *is* a new beginning for Bryan," Rick reminded her. "He's away from whatever circumstances got him into this situation. He *can* start over, if he wants to. It's the same for you and Noah, isn't it? It doesn't really matter what brought you here. What matters is what you do with this opportunity."

She studied him until they heard the sound of footsteps in the hall.

"Rick, you're home," a warm voice said. A slim, obviously pregnant woman embraced him, then turned to Cassie. "I'm Sara Loness," she said stretching out a hand. "I'm the head cook. Welcome to Lives."

"Thank you. I'm Cassie Crockett." Cassie shook Sara's hand then nudged Noah who finally rose. "This is my son, Noah."

After Sara greeted Noah, Rick explained what had just happened.

"Poor Bryan. I'll make sure supper doesn't have a lot of sugar," Sara assured him.

"And you should probably keep those away from him," Rick said, eyeing the platter of cinnamon buns on the counter. "But not from me."

"Why is it some people can eat whatever they want and never gain an ounce?" Sara smiled at Cassie. "I made extras," she said to Rick as she set plates and forks on the table.

"Thanks." Rick nudged Noah to the table then held Cassie's chair. Rick took note of the fact that Cassie startled a bit when his hand accidentally brushed her shoulder.

"I thought I saw a skating rink outside," Cassie said, her voice betraying nothing.

"Sara's husband, Kyle, made it. He's just coming in." Rick waited until his friend entered the kitchen. Then he introduced Cassie and her son. "Kyle's the activities director at Lives. He and I are teaching the kids hockey. It fosters cooperation, patience, a whole host of things." Rick suddenly felt restless under Cassie's scrutiny, as if he was being assessed for something, though he couldn't imagine what.

"Want to join us?" Kyle asked Noah.

"I n-never p-played hockey," Noah muttered.

"Between Rick and Kyle, who are the biggest hockey addicts in the world, you'll soon learn," Sara teased. "Do you like milk with your cinnamon buns?" Noah's eager nod made her laugh. "So does Kyle. What about your mom?"

"Sh-she's on a d-diet so s-she won't g-get f-fat." Noah actually grinned when the others burst into laughter.

"Noah Crockett! I am not." Cassie flushed a rich red.

"Bad mistake, Noah, my man," Rick told him, laying a hand on his shoulder. "Let me give you some advice. Never mention the words *fat* or *diet* in the presence of a woman." He leaned over and whispered very loudly, "It makes them grumpy."

Cassie and Sara shared a look.

"Here come the rest of the boys," Sara said. "They were at a sledding party."

When the current residents trooped into the kitchen, Sara introduced Cassie and Noah. "These fine fellows are Barry, Rod and Peter," she said. "Michael and Daniel won't arrive until tomorrow and Bryan is upstairs with Laurel," she explained to the boys. "He's not feeling well. I suppose you're not hungry in the slightest after the sledding party."

As one they began to protest.

Sara grinned. "Yeah, dumb question. After you wash you can join us."

As they rushed to comply, Kyle left to answer the phone. Rick noted Noah hadn't engaged any of the other boys, simply nodding at the introduction and returning to his music.

Rick knew why. That stutter was going to cause problems.

The first time he'd spoken to Noah he'd felt a familiar nudge in his heart. Experience told him that was God's prodding and it meant he was to help Noah. But how?

A moment later he had his answer.

When Sara disappeared inside the walk-in cooler leaving them alone, Rick decided to sound out Cassie while her son was still involved in his music, before the others returned.

"Noah told me his dad killed himself," he murmured. "That must have been very hard for you."

Her whole body dropped as if he'd settled a weight on her shoulders. Silence stretched between them. Finally Cassie spoke.

"Very hard, but harder on Noah, I think."

"If there's anything I can do to help," he offered.

It was obvious Cassie struggled to accept his offer. But after a long moment, she nodded.

"There might be."

"Just name it," he said.

"Would you be able to talk to Noah the same way you talked to Bryan?" Cassie asked in a hushed voice. "He's been hurting, trying to understand why his father would do that. I can't seem to reach him. But you might, the way you did with Bryan."

Rick's heart swelled with compassion for this mother's hurting heart.

"Please?" she whispered.

"I don't know that it will make any difference, Cassie, but I promise I'll do whatever I can to help Noah," Rick said, just before the other boys burst into the kitchen. He leaned closer. "The offer is open to you, too, if you want."

She shut down—there was no other way to express it. "Thank you, but I don't talk about the past. I appreciate whatever you can do for Noah, though."

It was a warning. *Back off.* And yet as he sipped the coffee Sara had served him, Rick knew he was going to have a hard time doing that. Her husband's suicide had affected her whether she admitted it or not. He had a hunch that refusing to discuss it was doing just as much damage to her spirit as it was to Noah's.

Don't get involved, his brain chided again.

She's hurting, his soul answered. *Am I not here to help others? How else can I make amends for my past?*

His brain was ready with a retort.

Is it only amends you want to make? Aren't you also trying to impress her?

His conscience reminded him that he needed to keep his motives clear, to focus on his mission.

He lifted his head and found a pair of beautiful brown eyes watching him.

Staying focused on his goal definitely wasn't going to be easy.

Chapter Three

"What's wrong, Rick?" Lucy Clow demanded on Saturday morning.

The diminutive septuagenarian, retired missionary and acting church secretary laid a model airplane kit on his desk.

"What's that?" he asked instead of answering.

"Vacation Bible School crafts for next summer, if you approve. I bought a ton of airplane kits online." Wispy tendrils of Lucy's snow-white hair straggled across her furrowed brow.

"Cool. Thanks for thinking ahead." Rick loved this woman's heart for God's work. "You've been poking at your hair again,"

"Forget my hair." The way Lucy clapped her hands on her hips made it clear he wouldn't escape her question. "Tell me what's eating you."

"Noah Crockett." Rick leaned back in his chair. "He's closed himself off. I promised his mother I'd help him, but I'm not making much progress."

"With his mother?" Lucy laughed at his expression and sat on a nearby chair. "There's nothing wrong with being attracted to someone, Rick."

"You know I can't get involved that way with a woman, Lucy. I've told you about my vow to God."

"I know what you promised God. I'm just not sure He asked for or even wanted your promise." Lucy frowned at him. "You keep beating yourself up over the past when God's already forgiven you. How is that any different from Noah acting out and staying aloof?"

"Noah hasn't hurt hundreds of people with his greed. I have. I thought I was too smart to get caught in a Ponzi scheme. That guy took all the money I handed over and instead of investing it, he used it to pay off his old clients." He groaned at his colossal ego. "Who else but an arrogant, materialistic creep would write a know-it-all book on how to beat the system and then lose his clients' money as well as his own to a slick-talking salesman?"

"God forgave you, Rick," Lucy murmured. "Forgive yourself."

"I can't." He sipped his now-cold coffee. "Not when that stupid book keeps selling and there's not a thing I can do to stop it."

"I noticed the royalty check when I deposited the offering last week," Lucy murmured. "I suppose that's what brought your guilt rushing back."

"It's never left," he muttered. "If only they'd stop selling that book." His hands fisted at his helplessness. "I feel that there are still people who are losing everything because of me."

"I guess you could always write another book against those practices."

"I can't." He shook his head then raked his fingers through his hair. "The agreement I signed doesn't allow me to contradict anything I wrote or reveal myself as the author."

"It's in God's hands, Rick." Lucy's quiet voice brimmed with comfort. "Leave it there."

"I'm trying. Anyway, it's not me we're talking about. It's Noah." He sighed. "Under that 'Who cares' attitude is a simmering cauldron of anger. I promised Cassie I'd help him, but he won't confide in me. He keeps burying himself in his music."

"I was practicing the piano for Sunday service while he was waiting for you yesterday," Lucy said thoughtfully. "He sat in the back and pretended to ignore me, but I heard him hum along. A couple of times he even sang a line. The kid has a pretty good voice."

Rick froze as an idea bloomed.

"You look funny." Lucy reached into her pocket. "I've got some pills for indigestion—"

"Lucy!" Rick hooted with laughter. "You, my dear secretary, are a genius."

"I tell Hector that all the time." She frowned at him. "But why am I a genius today?"

"Music." He kissed her cheek. "I'm going to start a kids' choir, Lucy, and I'm going to ask Noah to join. Will you play for us?"

"Me?" Lucy wrinkled her nose. She held out her fingers, bent with the ravages of arthritis. "I can't play that fast kids' stuff very well, Rick, but I guess I could help until you find someone else."

"Bless you." Rick grabbed his coat and gloves. "I'm going out to Lives to ask Laurel and Cassie if the boys can join. Then we'll put out the word all over town." He pulled open the door of his office then turned back and hugged the tiny woman. "You're a peach, Luce."

He was almost out the door when Lucy muttered, "I'd rather be a genius."

"You're both," he called.

As he gunned his snowmobile and headed out of town toward Lives, his heart raced with excitement. As he went, he prayed, *Let this choir be a blessing, Lord. Let Your word through music touch the kids' hearts and souls with healing. Especially Noah's. And Cassie's, too.*

Invigorated, he began formulating a list of songs that might help Noah face his anger. Once at Lives, Rick jumped off his machine and rapped on the door. When no one answered immediately he rapped harder. Finally the door opened a crack, revealing Cassie's tousled head and bleary-eyed face.

It wasn't lost on him that his heart beat a bit faster at the sight of her. But he ignored that fact as best he could.

"Hi." Rick blinked, checked his watch and winced. "I'm guessing you weren't up yet?"

"It's Saturday, Rick. Barely past nine. And it's New Year's Eve. We're all sleeping in." She smothered a yawn and opened the door wide. "But I'm up now. Come in."

"Sorry. I didn't think of the time," he apologized, his brain busy admiring the robe she wore. Delicately crocheted, it began in pale aqua at the bottom and grew progressively darker, drawing the eye up to where it turned a rich emerald tone in the lacy collar framing her face. "You look lovely."

"Nice of you to say, Rick, but I had my first shift at the hospital and worked till four this morning. I don't think 'lovely' applies." Cassie turned to get the coffee container out of the fridge.

"I do." He saw her pause a moment before she continued setting the perc. She flicked a switch and a moment later the rich fragrant aroma filled the room. "I'm really sorry I woke you."

"It must be important." She perched on a stool in the corner. "Do you want me to get Laurel?"

"Not yet. Though I do want to get her permission, and yours," he added.

"For what?" she asked around another yawn.

"For Noah and the boys to join a choir, a *kids'* choir," he emphasized.

Cassie tilted her head to one side. "Noah used to sing in a choir at home—" She stopped. "If he's interested I'm all for it."

"Hi, Rick." Laurel leaned against the door frame, glancing from him to Cassie. "All for what?"

"My kids' choir," he told her, noticing how tired she looked. "I wanted to ask your permission for the Lives boys to join, but we can talk later."

"Good because at the moment my brain is mush. I stayed up too late working on my taxes. Teddy Stonechild has me convinced I'm doing something wrong." She blinked sleepily. "If you'll excuse me I'm going to return to my dream life on a tropical beach. Good night—I mean morning." She waved a hand and left.

"Teddy was here?" Rick asked as Cassie poured coffee for both of them.

"Last night. Cream?" She held up the jug.

"Thanks." Rick nodded when she'd added the right amount. "I didn't realize he was back."

"Back? He doesn't live in Churchill?" This time Cassie sat directly across from him.

"His real home is in Vancouver. But he visits Churchill a lot." Rick savored the delicious brew. "Your coffee is fantastic. Much better than the slough water I had at the church."

"Do you live there?"

"Almost." He chuckled. "The church has a small manse. It's cozy." He refocused.

"Teddy's an interesting character. What else do you know?" she said.

"Kyle told me Teddy came as a client for his dad's tour business years ago and has kept coming ever since. I believe Teddy owns a hotel business that his son now runs."

Cassie nodded, then tilted her head to one side. "So what's the inspiration behind this choir of yours?"

Rick hesitated to broach the subject on his mind. "I've talked to Noah a couple of times."

Cassie perked up. "And?"

"I think he wants to open up but doesn't know where to start," he said. "Is there anything you can share with me that would help me understand what he's going through?"

"Like what?" Rick could see Cassie's barriers go up again, and he knew he had to tread very lightly.

"Maybe if I knew some details about what happened, I could make him feel that he could confide in me."

"I don't discuss my past, Rick." Her lips pinched firmly together. "I just want to forget."

"I understand." Rick could almost feel the pain emanating from Cassie, and he was caught off guard by how much he wanted to ease it. "Losing your husband must have been very difficult. I'm not trying to pry. But can't you tell me something? For Noah's sake?"

Cassie sat silent for several minutes, motionless, her gaze locked on something Rick couldn't see. Finally she took a sip of her coffee. Cradling the mug between her palms she gave a huge sigh.

"What do you want to know?"

"Anything you think will help Noah." Rick

waited, silently praying until finally she spoke again in a cool, matter-of-fact voice.

"My husband's name was Eric. I married him thirteen years ago, when I was eighteen. He was twenty-seven. He died two years ago. He drove on an icy street at high speed. Deliberately. He hit a tree and died."

Rick fought to keep his reaction to Cassie's horrific story as neutral as possible, for her sake. Now he understood her discomfort on the icy ride to Lives from the train.

"Do you mind telling me why Eric did it?" he asked gently.

"He was an accountant. He served on our church board and agreed to be board treasurer, to oversee a fund-raising campaign to build a new church." Cassie looked at him, her brown eyes guarded. "Eric was supposed to invest the building fund in something the board had chosen."

Cassie's voice broke and she paused to regain her composure. When she did, she said, "But Eric had other plans for the money. Plans I never knew much about." She frowned. "The congregation was excited about getting a facility that would give them room to expand their programs. Eric received a lot of phone calls from people wanting to know when there would be enough money to start building."

Compassion filled Rick. The way she avoided looking at him told him he was causing her pain by asking her about the past. Yet he needed information in order to help.

"Was that when Noah's stutter began?" he asked. "After his father died?"

Cassie shook her head, her eyes pleading with him not to make her say any more.

"I only want to help him, Cassie. Whatever you tell me is in strictest confidence, but I need to know," he said. Without thinking, he slid his hand across the table, over hers.

For a few moments Rick was certain she would tell him to forget it, that she didn't want to talk anymore. But she looked at him for a long time, and Rick held her gaze. Gradually her shoulders relaxed and her brown eyes lost their dark anger. She slowly pulled her hand away and exhaled.

"Tell me," he murmured.

"Noah's stutter started quite a while after his dad died, after everyone in the church turned on us when they discovered the money was gone," she said tiredly. "I became their scapegoat and Noah, too. The kids at school tormented him, called him the son of a thief." Tears formed on her thick golden lashes. "Noah was a total innocent. We both were. But when I tried to explain, no one would listen. To them we were as guilty as Eric. Noah's friends dumped him, parroting the nasty ugliness of what their parents said. That's when he began to stutter."

"Cassie, I'm so sorry." Rick hated the tears streaming down her lovely face. Holding her was folly, but how could he not offer her comfort?

He stood and moved to sit next to her, taking her in his arms slowly, gently, in case it wasn't what she wanted. He felt the tension break in her as she wept against his shoulder.

"They were Christians, Rick. They were supposed to love us."

"Yes, they were." How he wished he could ease this load from her. It broke his heart that her husband had caused so much grief and then abandoned her to face the consequences, that God's children had wreaked so much havoc on her son. "I'm sorry they didn't love you as Christ taught, Cassie. People are more important than lost money."

"Oh, they got their money." Cassie pulled out of his arms, dashing away her tears. Her voice grew harsh. "I sold the house and gave the money to the church to cover the loss."

She'd sold her home? Rick couldn't imagine what that decision had cost her, a single mom responsible for housing her child.

"I didn't do it because I felt guilty," Cassie said, her tone short. "I did it because I wanted them to stop torturing my son. But they didn't. They thought it wasn't enough, that I should cover the two years of interest they'd lost."

"But surely when you explained—"

"I stopped explaining," Cassie said, her voice passionless. "They displayed nothing but hatred for us. Before he ended it all, Eric tried to make it right. He sank every bit of our savings into trying to rebuild their fund. But he couldn't do it. So when he was gone, I found out there was no cushion for

Noah and me, no life insurance, nothing but my part-time nursing salary to support us."

"Your parents couldn't help?"

"My mother died when I was nine. Ever since then my father has been…busy." Cassie's voice dropped. "He blamed me, too, for not knowing what Eric was doing. So I stopped trying to defend myself."

Rick could see how much it cost Cassie to say this. He longed to pull her back into his arms, but for a moment, he questioned his motives. Did he want to offer her more comfort or did he simply love the feel of her in his arms? He wasn't sure he wanted the answer to that question.

"The day Noah got beaten up by his former friends was the day I knew getting him more counseling wouldn't help. We had to leave." Her eyes were dark beneath her damp eyelashes. "But leaving hasn't helped. I can't get him to let go of his anger."

"We'll figure out a way," Rick assured her. "Don't worry, Cassie. Once the two of you are involved in our church groups—"

"I won't be involved in them." She looked at him with an iciness that dared him to argue. "I can't be in a church, near people who call themselves Christians, without having it all come rushing back."

"These are not the same people, Cassie."

"But it's the same God. Where was He when my son—my *innocent* son—was being bullied? Why didn't He help us?" She glared at him, demanding answers.

"He did help you. He led you here," Rick murmured. "To a new life and a chance to start over."

"I will start over," she said with a nod. "But I don't intend to make the same mistake twice. I will not trust God again. It's too hard when He fails to come through."

"Cassie—"

"Don't." She shook her head. "I know what you're going to say. It's the same thing my father said to me. *Jesus never fails.*"

"It's true."

"In my case it isn't." Cassie held up a hand. "Don't trot out any more verses, Rick. I'm a preacher's kid. I've heard them all. But I don't believe in them. Not anymore."

So much pain. Rick knew he had pushed Cassie to her limit, and now it was time to back off.

"I'm sorry."

"So am I." She emptied her cup in the sink then turned to face him, her voice hard. "I hope you've heard enough to figure out how to help Noah because I don't intend to talk about this ever again."

"I appreciate your confiding in me," he told her quietly.

"If Noah wants to sing in your choir, I have no objection. If he wants to attend your church, that's also fine." The gold in Cassie's brown eyes flashed. "But don't expect me to do the same. Despite my father's admonitions about fleeing the fold, and any rebuke you might want to add, I will not be part of your congregation, Rick. Now, excuse me. I need to change."

Cassie swept out of the room and in that instant Rick's heart rate ripped into skyrocketing overdrive.

He suddenly realized why her face seemed so familiar.

Rick had seen a photo of a young Cassie every time he'd visited John Foster, the minister who'd saved him countless times while he was living on the streets, and who'd mentored him on his path to salvation and helped him get into seminary.

John carried a picture of Cassie in his wallet, and had a larger one on his desk. Sometimes Rick had come upon him staring at her photo, murmuring a prayer for her.

If he was honest, Rick had to admit he'd also been a little resentful of Cassie. She had a real home, a fantastic father who loved her, people who took care of her and made sure she was safe.

It had seemed to Rick that Cassie had everything and he had nothing. No family, no permanent address, no one who cared if he came or went. Even worse, there was no one to soothe his hurts. Oh, how he'd longed for that.

Rick wasn't sure how it had happened but the more he saw Cassie's photo, the more he'd stared at it, until he'd begun imagining a future in which he had all the things she did—a home, a family and love.

Funny thing was, as he and John deepened their friendship, Rick began to understand how deeply the caring father mourned the fact that he wasn't able to be with his daughter as much as he wanted. And why hadn't he?

Because John had been spending his time with Rick trying to help him find a way out of his life on the streets.

One more thing Rick had to feel guilty about.

His soul groaned under the weight of it.

When Cassie finally returned downstairs, the house was bustling and Rick was gone.

"L-look, Mom," Noah said, excitement glowing in his blue eyes. "It's s-snowing like c-crazy."

"Sure is," she agreed after a glance out the window. "Does this mean the fireworks for tonight are canceled?" she asked Laurel.

"Rick said he thought they would be. He's gone to set up a post at the church in case anyone gets caught in the storm and needs refuge." She smiled. "He's always thinking of others."

"P-Pastor R-Rick is going to s-start a choir," Noah told her. "He a-asked me to j-join."

"That sounds like fun." Cassie held her breath, unwilling to show any hope that he would get involved in something with his peers. "Do you think you will?"

"M-maybe. I l-like singing."

"Good." Cassie exchanged a nonchalant glance

at Laurel, knowing she'd understand. "So what will we do for New Year's Eve?"

"I'm glad you asked," said Cassie's friend.

Laurel already had a list of things she needed to prepare so the boys would enjoy their evening despite the fireworks cancellation. Cassie was glad to keep busy, hoping it would keep her mind off her conversation with Rick, when she'd dumped her past all over him, wept on his shoulder and then told him she'd never darken the door of his church.

She felt stupid, weak and ashamed that he'd seen her so needy, but being in his arms had felt wonderful.

Though Sara and Kyle were away for the holiday, Sara had left the freezer and cooler well stocked. Cassie and Laurel chose two casseroles and set them to bake for dinner, then prepared snack foods for later in the evening. They were putting the finishing touches on a series of sweet treats when the power went off.

"I was afraid this would happen with that high wind," Laurel said when it hadn't come back on after twenty minutes. "I need to go out to the shed and start the generator so the furnace will keep us warm."

Cassie watched her bundle up, unable to stem her worry. She stood at the window in the front hall and tracked Laurel through the whirling snow to make sure she arrived safely. But when minutes turned into half an hour and Laurel hadn't come back, worry burgeoned into fear. She'd just put on her coat to follow her friend when she saw Laurel pushing her way back through the drifts.

Cassie glanced at the light in the hall. The bulb remained unlit.

Apprehension filled her, but she tried to hide it as she met Laurel at the door. Once her friend was safely inside she quickly shut out the wind and snow.

"What's wrong?" Cassie asked quietly.

"I can't get it to start, though I tried about a hundred times." Laurel shivered as she rubbed her hands together. "Kyle tested it last week. It should be fine."

"So what do we do now?" Cassie whispered.

"I don't know," Laurel admitted. "We have to have heat so I'm going to read the manual again. Maybe I missed something." She hurried to her office.

Cassie stood in the hall. She wrapped her arms around her waist and shivered, trying to fight off her fear.

"M-mom, Laurel's c-cell phone is r-ringing," Noah bellowed from the kitchen.

Cassie answered. Her heart jumped a beat when she heard Rick's voice.

"Hey, Cassie. I tried the landline but I couldn't get through," he told her. "Is everything okay?"

"The power's out," Cassie murmured, keeping her voice low so the boys wouldn't guess from her tone how vulnerable she felt. "I guess that took out the phones."

"You haven't started the generator yet?" Rick sounded puzzled.

"Laurel tried. It won't start." Cassie went to Laurel's office but didn't find her there. "Laurel's not available right now. I'll have her call you." She didn't want to keep him when he must have things to do, but the sound of his voice was so reassuring.

"I contacted the power utility. A line is down. Apparently it will be a while before power will be restored." Rick paused for a moment. "But you guys need heat and that means the generator. I'm coming out there."

"In this storm?" Cassie glanced outside. Fear tiptoed along her spine. "It's too big a risk."

"Not at all. I know the landmarks along the way. I won't get lost," he assured her. "Besides, Kyle's taught me all the wilderness survival techniques he knows." He paused a moment. "I can't just leave you there, knowing you're in trouble."

"But it's so dangerous to travel in a storm."

"It's nice of you to worry about me, Cassie, but I'll be fine." His warm voice eased some of her concern. "See you in a bit."

"Please be careful," she whispered.

"Always."

Cassie hung up, unable to stem her worry. So many things could happen to Rick.

To keep herself busy, she set the table and mixed up a salad, trying to maintain her facade that nothing was wrong until Laurel decided how she wanted to explain the situation to the boys. A few moments later Laurel returned, having taken a second shot at fixing the generator. Cassie filled her in on Rick's call.

"I tried to talk him out of it but he insisted," she told Laurel helplessly.

"He would. That's the kind of man he is. Always giving for others." Worry showed clearly in Laurel's frown. "Can you keep the boys busy? I'm going to pray for Rick."

"I hope it works," Cassie told her.

"Prayer always works, Cassie. God always hears us. Romans says, 'Anyone who calls upon the name of the Lord will be saved.'" Laurel gave Cassie a quick smile before she left the room.

Cassie wasn't as certain as Laurel about God's protection, but she'd had enough conversation about God for one day.

Lives got chillier as the day went on. Laurel explained their predicament to the boys, who grew increasingly more solemn as they waited for Rick. Though it was barely mid-afternoon, the light was fading fast. Cassie knew that Rick's chances of arriving safely during the storm dropped considerably with every minute that passed.

When the last of the day's light faded, Cassie and Laurel raided Kyle's cupboard for emergency lanterns, which the boys began cranking. Then Cassie asked them to cut used milk jugs into candleholders.

"Wh-what are they f-for?" Noah asked.

"We'll put them in the windows so Rick can

find us in the storm." It was silly, but Cassie couldn't suppress her desperation to do something, anything, to help Rick reach them. Surely God wouldn't let anything happen to His emissary, would He?

He let other things happen.

Her heart squeezed tight at the foreboding that filled her. Cassie began to wish she could pray. But she couldn't get the words past the distrustful block in her throat. God had let her down before. How could she trust Him now, with something as important at Rick's life?

Then, above the whine of the raging wind, she heard the roar of a snowmobile. Her heart surging with relief, Cassie followed Laurel and the boys to the front door where they all urged Rick inside.

"What is this, an honor guard?" he joked, dragging off his helmet.

Everyone laughed, shattering the tension. Laurel urged the boys to go back to their warm quilts in the family room while Cassie helped Rick slide off his snow-covered coat. When his green eyes met hers, her heart beat so fast all she could manage was, "Welcome."

Cassie didn't think she'd ever been so glad to see someone in her entire life.

"Awful night to host a party." Rick tossed her a brash grin then kicked off his boots. Cassie and Laurel followed him as he hobbled to a kitchen chair and rubbed his toes. "Sorry it took so long. I made a wrong turn. Kyle will ream me out when

I tell him," he said, looking slightly abashed. "Thanks for lighting those candles. Believe it or not, they helped."

"That was Cassie's idea." Laurel turned to wink at her.

"Thank you, Cassie. I appreciate it." Rick's gaze clung to hers a bit too long before he turned back to Laurel. "Give me a few minutes to get the ice off my feet and I'll go check on the generator. I brought some extra gas for it in case you're low."

"We have lots of gas. I just can't get the thing to start," Laurel complained.

Cassie smiled as the boys returned and gathered around Rick, drawn in by his charisma. Wrapped in their warm blankets, they sat on the floor at his feet, asking a thousand questions, barely waiting for answers.

Rod had been at Lives the longest and had beaten Rick at checkers many times. Bryan had begun to adapt to his diabetes, thanks to Rick's encouragement. Barry was the quiet one, but his adoration of the young pastor was clear. Michael suffered from depression and Daniel dealt with the aftereffects of drug use. The newest arrivals were still finding their way at Lives, but as Rick laughed and joked with them, each boy joined in.

Every so often Rick's eyes lifted in search of hers. Each time Cassie pretended to be busy, too aware of her heightened response to him, too embarrassed by the surge of relief that had filled her when he'd walked through the door.

"Okay, I'm ready," Rick said to Laurel as he rose. "Got a couple of flashlights?"

She handed them to him. "I'm coming, too," she said. "I need to see what's wrong."

"Okay. See you guys in a bit," he said cheerfully. With a smile that seemed to be just for Cassie, he and Laurel left.

Cassie wasted the next ten minutes telling herself she would have worried about anyone who had been out in a storm like this. By the time the power flickered on, she'd almost convinced herself it was true. But when Rick returned and accepted the hot chocolate she handed him, her heart was still thudding and she couldn't catch her breath.

With the furnace blasting out heat, Lives quickly warmed up. Cassie and Laurel finished preparing supper using candlelight to save the generator because no one knew when power would be restored. Then they all gathered around the big table to eat.

Cassie was not surprised in the slightest that Rick made the meal joyful, from his grace of thanksgiving to the jokes he shared.

"He's got the boys so busy laughing there's no time for them to miss their families," Laurel said as they cleaned up the kitchen. "Just another reason I adore that man."

Laurel coaxed Rick into leading the games she'd planned, and Cassie couldn't help but laugh when he refused to let either of them sit out, despite their protests. Cassie didn't mind. The room resounded with loud and happy laughter and she couldn't remember when she'd had so much fun. Even Noah seemed to lose his reticence, begging her to join in a game of Twister that left Cassie feeling like a pretzel.

"You're good at this," Rick told her, offering a helping hand up. When she took it, she felt the warmth of his hand against hers.

"I have to be—it's Noah's favorite." Once on her feet, she let go of his hand, anxious to break the connection between them.

What was wrong with her tonight? Were her responses so strong because she'd been afraid for Rick?

"It's getting close to midnight," Rick said. "Maybe we should fill the punch glasses so we'll be ready for a toast."

Since the others were busily arranging the white domino tiles for a game, Cassie agreed. She and Rick worked together. After their hands touched for the third time, Cassie couldn't remain silent.

"I was so scared for you," she said in a half whisper so the boys wouldn't hear.

"Really?" His eyes widened. A smile stretched across his face. "That was nice of you. I don't think I've ever had anyone worry about me before."

A pleased look stayed with him even after they'd finished filling the glasses. Such a small thing, yet he seemed delighted by it. Cassie couldn't help wondering why this handsome and very nice man didn't have anybody who cared about him.

Soon they were finished and all was ready for the midnight hour.

"One more minute," Rick said, smiling. "Then we start a new chapter in our lives." He tapped a spoon against a glass. "Hey," he called. "Are you guys ready for our New Year's toast?"

The boys grabbed their glasses, laughing as they counted down the seconds. Her mind working furiously, Cassie moved as far as possible from Rick. She could not, would not get caught next to him at the stroke of midnight. Her cheeks warmed at the thought of his lips touching hers and she scolded herself for her imagination. But when she caught his gaze she knew that he'd been thinking along the same lines, and that flustered her even more.

"Ready?" she asked Noah, tearing her gaze from Rick's.

"Y-yeah." He blinked as Laurel's big wall clock chimed the midnight hour.

"Happy New Year!" Cassie clinked her glass with her son's. "May it be your best year ever, Noah."

"Happy N-New Year," he repeated.

The boys moved around, eager to tap their glasses against everyone else's. That was how Cassie ended up next to Rick, despite her best efforts.

"Happy New Year, Cassie," he said softly.

It was only their glasses that made contact, but the effect was the same as if his lips had touched hers. She spilled a few drops of punch on her fingers as she tried to find her voice.

"Happy New Year," she whispered.

His eyes held hers for a long timeless moment. Finally he turned toward the boys and led them in singing "Auld Lang Syne." Cassie forced herself to breathe in and out slowly, causing her heart rate to eventually return to normal by the end of his short but fervent prayer asking God to bless each of them in the year ahead.

"Let's share our resolutions," Rick said.

"What's a resolution?" Rod asked.

"Grab your snacks. We'll sit in the family room," Laurel said. "Rick can explain."

Cassie sat on the arm of the sofa beside Noah and waited until everyone had settled, curious to hear what Rick would say.

"Resolutions are plans we make to accomplish specific things in the coming year," he explained in a solemn tone. "It's a goal to focus on. For example, my resolution this year is to serve God with all my heart, even when it means sacrificing my own plans."

Cassie frowned. The way Rick said it made it sound as if he was trying to make up for something. What was her resolution?

"What about you guys? Any idea what you'd like to accomplish in the new year?"

Rod grimaced. "My resolution is to figure out math."

"That's a good one," Rick encouraged. "Hard, but good. Anyone else?"

"Mine is to get another saxophone," Michael said, his blond curly head tilted to one side.

"You play sax? You and I could brainstorm on that maybe," Rick offered.

"I'd like that," he said shyly.

Cassie was surprised Michael had answered at all. According to the file she had on him, he was suffering from depression. He certainly hadn't volunteered any information previously. It must be Rick who was helping him find his place.

"I'm going to get along better with others this year," Laurel said.

Soon Rick had coaxed each boy to talk about some plan for the future—everyone except Noah, who'd said only that he'd think about it. Cassie's heart was still aching from Noah's withdrawal, so she was not prepared when Rick called her name.

"What's yours, Cassie?" Rick's gaze pinned her.

"My resolution?" She blinked in surprise, though she knew she should have expected the question. But what to say?

Like a giant wave, the hurt rolled over her, lending a sharp edge to her voice when she said, "I'm going to rebuild my life this year."

Rick studied her for several moments. Was that pity in his eyes? Cassie did not want pity from this man. She shifted uncomfortably, aware that the boys were now staring, too.

"Well, you're in the right place, Cassie, because that's what we do at Lives Under Construction, right, boys?" Laurel said, kindly drawing the attention away from her.

"Thank you all for sharing," Rick added. "I'll pray God will help each of you fulfill the desires of your hearts."

In the clamor of the next hour of games, Cassie often felt Rick's eyes on her. She studiously avoided looking at him, forcing herself to join the fun, suppressing all that she was feeling. But when her eyes accidentally met his, she knew she wasn't fooling him.

When the boys could no longer hide their yawns, Laurel said it was time for bed. She convinced Rick to sleep in the family room because of the storm, and then Cassie persuaded Laurel to leave the cleaning-up to her.

She'd just snapped off the kitchen light and was about to go to her room when Rick's touch on her arm stopped her. She shifted so his hand dropped away. "Yes, Rick?"

"I wanted to wish you the very best with your resolution, Cassie." His green eyes swirled with something she couldn't define, something that made her knees weak against her will. "I hope God will bless you and Noah as you start a new life here. I'll pray you find what you need in Churchill and at Lives."

"Thank you. Happy New Year to you, too, Rick," she said quietly. "Thanks for coming to our rescue."

She wanted to say good-night and go, and yet

somehow she couldn't leave. Time stood still, holding her immobile for several long moments, unable to leave. Finally he spoke.

"Good night, Cassie. God bless."

Cassie turned and left the room, almost running in her haste to escape the rush of emotions that filled her. She sat on her bed, staring out the window at the storm that was no match for the private storm raging inside her, thanks to the way Rick had looked at her.

What was that she'd seen in his eyes? Was it pity? Sorrow? Need?

What did the handsome pastor want from her?

Perhaps that was the wrong question. Perhaps instead, she should be asking what did *she* want from him?

Chapter Four

A week later Rick accepted a refill of coffee from the waitress at Common Ground, the town's favorite coffee shop, suddenly aware that he'd been admiring the way Cassie's gold sweater accented her eyes for way too long. Those brown eyes had captivated him from the first time he'd seen that childhood picture in her dad's office. He should have told her up front that he knew her father, but guilt held him back. He was part of the reason she didn't get to spend time with her father.

Not only that, but imagining Cassie's disgust if she knew about his past, the whole ugly story, made him hold his tongue.

"I'm glad I spotted you in here, Cassie. Doubly glad you invited me to share coffee with you. I've been wondering how Bryan's doing keeping track of his blood sugar levels."

That wasn't what he'd wanted to talk about at all, but he couldn't just blurt things out.

"There hasn't been an overnight change. I still have to remind him periodically to check. But he's getting better at taking responsibility," she said quietly. "We haven't had any more incidents like the day he arrived."

"Great. That's progress." Rick paused. "And Noah?"

"He's had two days of school and it seems like he's wound tighter than ever," Cassie said. "I'm running out of ideas."

"I've been trying to reach Noah without being too obvious. So far, he's polite but closed up like a clam." Rick smiled, hoping to ease the furrow that marred her forehead. "But don't worry. I'm not giving up."

If only Rick could only find a way to help Cassie's son as her father had helped him, maybe he could make it up to Cassie for taking so much of her father's time.

"I know it's not easy. You're busy with your congregation." Cassie's eyes brimmed with hidden emotions, emotions that were just out of his reach. "I appreciate your taking time with him, Rick."

"He's a good kid. I enjoy talking to him. We've discovered we have a common interest in astronomy." Rick studied her. "How are you doing? Is the job at Lives what you expected?"

"It's much different than working in a hospital." She fiddled with her coffee cup. "Mostly working at Lives is a breeze."

"Mostly?" Rick leaned forward.

She smiled ruefully. "I've been trying to figure out how to help Michael. He struggles with seizures, you know. He needs an outlet to help him relax."

"Your mother's heart overtakes the nurse in you, doesn't it?" A rush of admiration swelled inside him.

Her cheeks pinked and she looked down, avoiding his scrutiny.

"All Michael talks about is his saxophone."

"Which is where?" Rick found himself admiring the way tendrils of her golden curls caressed the nape of her neck, and forced his eyes back to her face.

Cassie met his eyes. "I don't know."

"If you can find out when and where he last had it, maybe we could try to get it back. What do you think?"

"I think you're a good person to work with," Cassie murmured. "I'll ask him. Thank you for the suggestion."

"My pleasure." He swallowed the last of his coffee. "I've got to get going. Lucy promised she'd practice playing the choir music with me this afternoon. We plan to start up next week." He slid his arms into his jacket. "You are coming with the boys to the fireworks tonight, aren't you?"

"After all the buildup you've given it?" Cassie chuckled. "I wouldn't miss it."

Rick was trying to ignore the fact that she had

the most wonderful smile, which was probably why he spoke without thinking.

"Mind if I join you to watch them?"

When she didn't answer, he wondered if her silence meant she wanted to refuse. "You and the boys," he amended.

"The more the merrier." Cassie nodded slowly, as if she'd hunted for a way to get out of spending the evening with him and couldn't think of one. "But if as many people show up as you claim, it might be difficult to find us."

"With those rowdy boys in tow?" He shook his head and grinned. "Finding you will be a cinch." Rick decided he needed to have another chat with God, especially with regard to Cassie Crockett. He was getting too interested in her and that did not bode well for keeping his distance. "Can I ask you a question completely unrelated to Bryan?"

"I guess." She blinked, her confusion evident.

"You wear the most unusual sweaters. I've never seen anything like them. I wondered where you get them."

"This?" She plucked her sweater away from her midriff. "I made it."

"Really?" Surprise rendered him speechless as he imagined Cassie bent over knitting needles. His mental picture of a nurse was a steady, hardworking, earnest soul. Somehow he'd never thought of a nurse as artistic, yet the creativity displayed in her sweater showed a mind that loved beauty. It revealed yet another aspect of her that intrigued him.

"Why did you ask?" Cassie studied him with a certain probing look. Her "nurse" look, he'd dubbed it.

"There's a woman, Alicia Featherstone. She teaches native culture at Lives. She also has a store in town where she sells unique things to tourists and residents alike. Many native artists sell their work there." Rick noted the way her eyes flared in interest as she leaned forward.

"I'd like to see it. How do I get there?"

He described the location, then hesitated.

"What aren't you saying?" Cassie asked.

"I don't want you to think I'm nosy, but Alicia and I were both at Lives when you were at the hospital the other day. She admired a sweater much like the one you're wearing. Alicia's always looking for artists to stock her store so I thought you might want to sell some of your work. You did say you were hoping to earn some extra money," he added. "Alicia's great about taking things to sell on consignment, or so I've been told."

"She liked my sweater enough to want to sell it?" Cassie blinked. "Then I will definitely talk to her. Thank you." Her glance was turning into a stare. She flushed and dragged her gaze away. Feeling self-conscious, she grabbed her satchel off a nearby chair and withdrew the contents.

"What's that?"

"This is my current project. I took it to the hospital to work on during my break today."

It was going to be a sweater. Rick could discern

that much. But it seemed far too big for her. And in his opinion the taupe and beige tones were the wrong colors for her fair complexion.

"It looks complicated," he finally managed, unable to think of anything else.

"It is. It will look like this." She pulled a sketch from her bag and placed it on the table for him to see. Her fingers trembled a little as she smoothed it out. "I started it a while ago. It was going to be a Christmas gift for Eric."

Rick suddenly understood.

Cassie swallowed and visibly gathered herself. "But the yarn was very expensive and it seemed wrong to waste it. It's way too big for Noah, but I can always give it away."

"It's very fine work." His fingers seemed to reach out of their own volition to touch the length she'd already created. "It's nothing like the ones you make for yourself."

"No. I hand-dye my sweaters because I can never find anything bright enough." She laughed and the tension disappeared. "I'm afraid I'm addicted to color. Eric wasn't."

Her voice died away. She stared at the yarn she held, her face a misery. Rick couldn't stand to see it.

"You can talk about him, Cassie," he murmured. "You can tell me anything you want to."

"What do you mean?" She frowned at him, a wary glint in her eyes.

"I don't suppose it's easy to talk to Noah about

his father. Moms always want to help their kids think the best of their parents, even when it isn't always true."

Rick wasn't sure why he added that last part. It was something in Cassie's manner that made him wonder if there might have been something bad going on with Eric.

Or was he simply envying her because she'd found someone to share her life and he couldn't?

"I don't want to talk about Eric," she said firmly. Cassie stuffed her work back in her bag. "This is just a hobby."

"A hobby is a good thing to have up here when the days are short and the nights long and dark." The jewel tones she wore enhanced her natural beauty, but Rick didn't say that. Instead, he said, "Go talk to Alicia, Cassie. If nothing else, you'll find a friend."

"Maybe I'll go see her before I head back to Lives." When Cassie smiled—truly smiled—it dissolved the tension lines around her eyes and revealed the full extent of her beauty.

Rick cleared his throat. "I'd better get going. See you tonight."

As Rick left the restaurant, his head rang with a question—how could he escape the magnetizing lure of Cassie Crockett?

Did he really want to? His entire life he'd longed for someone special to help create the family he wanted. But he'd made that vow.

Until now, it hadn't been a problem. This was

the first time Rick had feelings for someone since then. The agonizing thing was, he could never act on them.

Cassie studied Rick's disappearing figure. The big picture windows allowed her to watch him saunter down the street, talking to everyone he met. A small, silver-haired woman met him at the church steps. Rick's face broke into a smile at something she said. Then he held out his arm and escorted her into the church.

Cassie finished her coffee and prepared to leave as her mind swirled with questions about Churchill's youngest minister. Rick had an amazing ability with people. *Please God, let him find a way to help Noah.*

As quickly as the prayer filled her brain, she pushed it away. God didn't answer. There was no point in asking.

Cassie was about to leave the coffee shop when someone said, "I've been wanting to talk to you. You're Cassie Crockett, the new nurse at Lives Under Construction. I'm Alicia Featherstone."

"It's nice to meet you."

"Let me pay for my coffee and then we can talk at my store. It's called Tansi—that's Cree for 'Hi, how are you?'"

"Oh." Startled that this woman knew her, Cassie found herself escorted down the street and into a small shop. There she became entranced by the assortment of crafts. "This is a wonderful place," she murmured in awe.

"Thank you." Laughter rang in Alicia's voice.

"Rick Salinger told me you were interested in my sweater."

"Oh, Rick—he's such a sweetie. I've never met anyone with a bigger heart." Alicia leaned forward. "I loved your sweater. I have a hunch you wear the one I saw at Lives, but I'd love to see what else you have."

"Right now, just this." Cassie set her bag on the counter and undid her coat before she lifted her work out of her bag.

"I love this scarf of yours." Alicia examined it more closely. "Anything else?"

"So far, just this." Cassie withdrew the sweater she'd planned for Eric. "It isn't finished yet, but this is what it will look like." She set the sketch on the counter beside her sweater.

After examining the sweater, Alicia slid it back into the bag. "Bring it in when it's done." Then she reached out to finger Cassie's scarf. "This is so beautiful. I love the color. Could you make six of these for me?"

"Yes, but the color won't be an exact match." Slightly dazed by the request, Cassie explained about her dying process and the need for hand-washing.

"We'll make a tag with those instructions." In a brisk tone, Alicia explained how she operated. "All your supplies are your responsibility. You tell me how much you need and we'll set a price, but you won't get paid until the item sells. Is that suitable?"

"It sounds fine." Bemused by the speed at which she'd found another job, Cassie nodded.

"Great!" Alicia grinned. "I'm glad Rick told me about you, Cassie. I'm going to love selling your work. Isn't he a great guy? We're lucky to have him in Churchill."

As Cassie listened to the other woman sing Rick's praises she wondered for a moment if there was something other than friendship between the two.

Then she reminded herself that it shouldn't matter to her. A wiggle of dismay filled her. She'd always suspected Rick must have someone who cared for him. He was too nice for it to be otherwise.

"Sometimes I think Rick and I are the only two single people in Churchill," Alicia joked. "We're both determinedly single so it's nice when more singles move to town. Welcome."

"Thanks." So Rick and Alicia weren't a couple. Why did she feel relief? "I'd better go get started on those scarves," Cassie said.

"You have wool already?"

"Several boxes of it." Cassie chuckled at Alicia's surprised face. "I brought it with me when we moved."

"Good. Come and have coffee with me sometime," Alicia offered.

"That would be fun. Thank you, Alicia. Bye."

As Cassie left, her heart sang at the chance to earn money to put in her meager savings account. Thanks to Rick—again. He was turning out to be a lifesaver in a lot of ways.

Her heart gave that funny bump of joy that warmed her inside whenever she thought of Churchill's young pastor.

Perhaps she should add her heart to the list of things she could no longer trust.

When Rick stopped by Lives just before the boys returned from school that afternoon, Cassie hid her smile. Judging by how often he'd arrived in time for meals, she thought it was pretty obvious the gregarious Rick hated eating alone. And, of course, this afternoon *was* hockey practice.

Rick was unbuttoning his coat as the boys trooped in, sniffing the air still redolent with Sara's freshly baked cookies. Cassie waited for Noah, hoping today had been a better day. When he finally strolled into the kitchen, her hopes took a nosedive. The right side of his face was red and swollen, particularly around his eye.

"What happened?" Cassie rose, wanting to enfold him in her protective arms but suppressing the urge, mindful of his glare of warning.

"I g-got h-hit b-by a b-ball." Noah clenched and unclenched his jaw. "H-here." He thrust an envelope toward her.

"You were playing ball in the snow? I see." Cassie read the explanation from the principal.

Your son was involved in an altercation. Neither child was seriously injured but we will be requiring him to do detention. It was signed by the principal. She glanced around. None of the other boys said a word and they looked everywhere but at her.

"The best thing for an eye like that is cold. Is there a bag of peas in the freezer?" Rick's apparent nonchalance reinforced her instinct that now was not the time to make a motherly scene.

"I'll check." Cassie took one more look at her son, then opened the freezer door while Rick carried carafes of hot chocolate and a platter of cookies to the table.

As her pregnancy progressed, Sara now frequently rested in the afternoon. Cassie chipped in to help as often as she could. Lucy Clow also appeared almost every day to help, as well as some other local women. Now Rick was pouring mugs of cocoa for the boys. He made no bones about helping out anywhere he was needed, Cassie noted. Including with her son.

"Mind if I share your snack, guys?" Rick asked. "I'm hungry."

"You're always hungry when you come here." Rod gave him a cheeky grin. "Don't ministers get paid? Can't they afford their own groceries? Or can't you cook?"

"The answers to your questions, in order, are yes, yes and a resounding yes. In fact, I am an expert cook. As you should know, since you've chowed down my fried chicken," Rick said in his own defense. "But it's no fun cooking for yourself. Besides, I'm not as good a baker as Sara is."

"Keep that in place for a few minutes," Cassie told Noah, pressing the bag of peas against his face as she regained her composure. "It should take down the swelling a little."

"S-stop f-fussing," Noah said in a harsh tone, exactly as Eric used to.

Cassie opened her mouth, caught Rick's warning glance and swallowed her response. She turned to refill her coffee cup while surreptitiously rubbing away the tear that had squeezed out the corner of her eye.

"She's not fussing, Noah. She's doing her job as a nurse and a mom," Rick gently corrected.

Cassie was grateful for his support. When she returned to her seat, Rick's eyes met hers with an intensity she couldn't avoid. A moment later Rick leaned over and whispered something in Noah's ear. Noah frowned, muttered "Thanks" to Cassie, then returned to his hot chocolate.

Cassie wondered what Rick had said.

"So, you guys have lots of homework?" Rick asked the group, lightening the tense atmosphere. "Probably won't have much time left to play hockey, will you?"

"You wish." Again Rod's sly grin appeared. "We got together at lunch hour and did most of it. Ten minutes or so and I'll be ready. You guys?"

The other kids nodded their agreement.

"And you, Noah? Are you going to be able to

play?" Rick asked. "Did you do your homework during lunch, too?"

The boy's quick flinch told Cassie all she needed to know but she said nothing, content to let Rick handle her recalcitrant son.

"No." Noah's sullen glare said it all.

"Oh. Right. You were hit by a ball. At lunch, huh?" Rick nodded then rose. "Too bad you have to miss practice today."

Noah made a face at Rick but there was no malice in it. Cassie felt a twitch of hope that maybe finally someone was finally reaching her son.

She would have liked to hug Rick for that, but that would be foolish. He was just being a nice guy. Still, she couldn't get used to it.

"Well, guys, I'll get my skates on and dig the equipment out." Rick put his used cup and plate in the dishwasher. "The Lord's given us a nice warm day."

"It's not what I'd call warm," Michael hooted in derision. "But at least it won't be too cold for the fireworks tonight."

"Good thing it's a Friday and you can stay up late," Rick said.

"Does that make a difference?" Cassie asked with a small smile. "It will be dark in half an hour. They could shoot the fireworks off before supper."

"Now what fun would that be?" Rick joked.

His teasing wink stopped her breath and any rebuttal she might have made. For one brief moment, she let herself imagine that she could relax her guard and trust Rick.

Rick smiled, his eyes focused and intently unnerving, as if he could see into her soul and read the questions and doubts that hammered at her. "I'll be ready whenever you are, guys," he said to the boys, then walked out of the kitchen.

It was several minutes before Cassie started breathing normally again.

"Don't you love fireworks?" Rick grinned at Cassie as the first boom resounded across Hudson Bay.

"Yes, I do. I wasn't allowed to see them when I was a kid. My father figured I'd be too tired the next day, though why he'd care I don't know. He was never home much to notice me."

Her memories about her father created a lump in his throat. Why hadn't he told her the truth days ago?

Cassie raised an eyebrow. "What's your excuse?"

"I need an excuse to enjoy this?" Rick gazed up at the light display to avoid looking into Cassie's eyes. "I don't have one, other than I get caught up in the dazzle of it all. When that powder goes off, all eyes get lifted up to the heavens and everything stops to admire its beauty." He murmured, "'The heavens are telling the glory of God; they are a marvelous display of His craftsmanship.'"

"Psalms 19." Cassie tilted her head upward. "I memorized that in girls' club years ago. So how did you get permission to stay up and watch them when you were young?"

Rick hesitated. He hadn't told her anything about his past yet. Maybe now was the time to start. "I was a street kid, so there wasn't anyone to tell me when to go to bed. Sometimes there wasn't a bed, actually," he said, attempting to joke. His voice sounded funny, even to his own ears.

He had to tell her he knew her father. How could he expect her trust if he wasn't honest? The absence of truth meant he'd essentially been lying to her and he didn't want to do that anymore.

"I didn't know that." Her voice brimmed with sympathy. "I always think the hardest thing in the world is for a kid to grow up without a family. What happened to yours? If you don't mind telling me," she added after a slight pause.

"It's not that I mind telling you, it's that I can't. I don't know what happened to them. I have no family." Saying it still hurt—he couldn't deny that. "At least none I know of. The only thing I remember is living on the street. Maybe I wiped it out, maybe it will come back someday, but all I know is that I grew up in Toronto."

"What's your first memory?" Rick noticed her gaze slide from the sky to Noah, then to him.

"It's not the first but it's my best one from those days. I was starving, panhandling to buy something to eat. A man handed me a couple of bucks then told me about his church. He said they had what you'd call a soup kitchen. The next day I went and

I loved it." Rick smiled at the memories. "The man was there. He welcomed me, acted as if I was the best thing since sliced bread. He made me feel worthwhile, important. Loved." He choked up at the word. It took a few moments for him to regain control. "He was the reason I kept going back."

"I'm glad you found him." Cassie peeked at him through her thick lashes. Rick knew this was the moment when he should tell her the truth, but somehow he couldn't seem to do it. He didn't want to see the hurt fill her eyes, eyes that he had come to know so well in such a short time.

"Me, too. Anyway, that church basement is my first really good memory." He touched her arm to draw her attention to the balls of blue sparks now exploding across the sky. "I don't remember how I knew I was Rick Salinger. I just knew."

"It must be hard not to know your history." The sympathy exuding from her warmed his soul like a healing balm.

"I can't say. I've only ever known that I was alone." He pretended it didn't matter, but he couldn't fool himself that the age-old ache to have a home of his own and a family who loved him wasn't still alive deep inside, despite his vow to sacrifice both.

In a flash Rick relived moments of sheer terror from his past: hiding from a gang, trying to stay awake so he wouldn't get mugged or beaten, or worse, friends dying from drug overdoses. A shiver ran through him at how close he'd come to losing his life. If not for God and Cassie's father—

"I'm sorry no one was there for you, Rick." Cassie must have seen through his pretense because her brown eyes grew soft. She touched his shoulder. "To be on your own at such a young age must have been terrifying. I wish I could erase the pain for you."

"Thank you. But after that first day at the church, I wasn't totally alone any longer. That man became a good friend."

Cassie's tenderness was almost Rick's undoing. No one except her father had ever expressed such compassion toward him and it overwhelmed him. As the light show continued to explode around them Rick gulped down the lump in his throat, grasping for composure. He couldn't tell her he knew her father now. Not when he was wasn't sure he could remain in control.

"How's Noah doing?" he asked, changing the subject.

"Okay, I guess." Cassie sighed. "He wouldn't say anything else about what happened with his eye but I don't think he got hit by a ball."

"No." Rick had suspicions, but for now that's all they were. He wouldn't say more until he was sure. He waited for her to continue, watching her stare across the snow-covered beach to where her son stood alone, apart from the other Lives' boys.

"His stuttering was worse today. That's usually a sign that he's bothered by something. He didn't say anything to you?" She peered at him through the flickering light shed by a bonfire behind them, higher up the beach.

Rick shook his head. Colored sparks flared in a river-fall of light across the ice. "Tell me about your childhood, Cassie."

"Not much to tell." She avoided Rick's stare, but he could sense that she had more to say.

Whether it was their isolation from everyone else that led her to confide in him or the intimacy that the semi-darkness seemed to offer, Rick wasn't certain. All he knew was that her next words seemed torn from her.

"After my mom died, my father was too busy with his ministry to bother much with me. I always suspected he wanted a son to follow in his footsteps, so I was probably a disappointment to him." Her words revealed a depth of hurt he guessed she usually kept hidden.

"I'm sure he loved you very much," Rick said, wanting to say more.

"Then how come he never came to my awards days or the father-daughter events?" she shot back. "How come he was always too busy to see me in the school play? How come he missed my school graduation?"

The ache underlying those words made Rick want to comfort her, to pull her into his arms again the way he had the night she'd told him about Eric. If he didn't feel so guilty, he probably would have.

"Forget it." Cassie inhaled a shaky breath, then

exhaled in a short sharp laugh. "I don't know why I told you that."

"Because you needed to say it." Rick settled for touching her shoulder as a means of trying to offer comfort.

"He'd apologize, say how terribly sorry he was that he'd been detained. That's what he always called it—detained. He always said he'd make it up to me, but how do you make up for lost special moments?" She shook her head. "I never understood how he could preach about responsibility to other people and yet abandon me."

"He didn't do it purposely." Cassie gave him a sharp glance, and Rick took a breath. This had gone on long enough. "Cassie, is your father John Foster?"

A blast of brilliant fireworks went off above their heads as Cassie gasped, "How did you know that?"

"I knew your dad," Rick finally admitted. "It was his church where I found solace. Your father is the one who welcomed me, fed me and got me out of scrapes more times than I can remember."

Cassie stared at him as if she couldn't comprehend what he was saying. "Well, at least he helped someone." Her raspy laugh wasn't covered by the racket from the explosives.

"Purposefully or inadvertently," Rick continued, trying to figure out the best way to salvage the situation, "we all hurt the ones we love, Cassie. But one thing I always knew about your dad—the thing all us kids knew—was how much John loved you." What was going on behind those stunned brown eyes of hers? "Remember I said you seemed familiar?"

"I thought it was a come-on," she rasped.

"No. I recognized you. I just couldn't remember why." Rick put both his hands on her shoulders. "Then I remembered. He carried your picture in his pocket and he showed it to everyone. He also had a photo of you in his office. He bragged about you all the time."

Cassie took a few steps away from Rick as if to process his words. Rick decided to just stop speaking for a moment, to let her get a grasp on what he was telling her.

"I can brag about Noah, but unless I'm there for him, it doesn't matter," she finally said.

"Cassie." Rick grasped her arm and turned her toward him. He pointed to his chest. "I'm one of the reasons he wasn't there for you."

When she spoke, her tone was scathing. "You don't have to make excuses for him."

"I'm not. Your dad was the man who welcomed me every time I went to his church. He's the one who made us street kids feel safe, wanted, even if it was just for as long as we were with him." He squeezed his eyes closed and whispered a prayer of thanks for the reprieve he'd been granted.

When he opened his eyes, Cassie had a hard look on her face.

"Your father made sure I had something to eat when I was so hungry my ribs touched my backbone and I didn't have money to buy anything to shoot up and take the pain away. He was the one who got me to talk about goals and dreams for the future and helped me see I could reach them. He helped me find a way to go to college." Rick inhaled and laid out the bare truth. "I'd be dead now if your dad hadn't come looking for me when I was teetering on the edge. He dragged me, kicking and screaming, into drug rehab. He refused to let me escape his love."

"My father isn't like that." Cassie's brows drew together.

"He was exactly like that, Cassie. He was the closest thing to a father I ever knew. Tough, demanding, but also fair-minded and loving," Rick insisted. "John made sure we had coats and gloves for the winter. He made sure we always had Christmas dinner and a gift of some kind, and then he'd tell us about God's gift to us." Guilt suffused Rick. "If he wasn't there when you wanted him, Cassie, it was because of me, because your dad was taking care of me."

"I can't believe this." She wrinkled her nose in disbelief, but her voice held an edge. "He never told me anything about this. Nor did his church staff, and I spent a lot of time with them."

"But that was John," Rick argued. "He wasn't into bragging. He just did what he thought was right." The anger on Cassie's face convinced him that he wasn't explaining things correctly. "When I was struggling to stay straight, I went to see your dad. He told me off, said there are no guarantees in life. You make a choice and you live with it. He picked up your picture and looked at it for a long time."

When Cassie glanced up at him, Rick couldn't help himself—he reached out and touched her hair as tears filled her eyes. "He said he loved you more than life itself, but he was afraid his choices had hurt you. I never knew what he meant until now."

Cassie stepped away from him again, needing space.

"John loves you, Cassie. Deeply. We all knew it and envied you for that love." Rick saw her flinch. "Maybe he spent too much time with us and his other church work, but that doesn't mean he didn't love you dearly."

"Really?" Cassie's eyes were ablaze with anger now. "Then why, after Eric's death, when I needed support against all the blame and accusations of my church, did my *loving* father tell me I needed to ask God's forgiveness? Why did he imply I was to blame for Eric's actions? Why didn't he at least offer to help us financially?"

"I don't have the answers," Rick said, helpless against her tide of anger. He wanted so badly to help her see John as he did—a loving, caring parent. And yet Rick knew there were no perfect parents. "Maybe you misunderstood what he was saying."

"Believe me, I got his message loud and clear."

Cassie stood rigid, apart, alone. "I got in the way of his 'calling.'"

Rick prayed for words to help her rebuild her relationship with her father. But all he could think about was the part he'd played in creating a barrier between the two of them.

"All I know for sure is that your father loves you, Cassie," he said in the stillness of the moment between bursts of fireworks. "And that kind of love doesn't change or die. Your dad loves you very much. But the time he should have spent with you, he spent talking to, helping me. It's my fault he wasn't there for you."

"If my father did something that helped you when you were a kid, I'm glad." Cassie's words were sharp, like ice crackling in the bay. "But nothing he did for you will make me forgive the pain and suffering he put me through then, or wipe out the way he, of all people, judged me for Eric's mistake."

"You might think you don't need your father in your life, but what about Noah?" Rick murmured.

"There is nothing my father could give Noah that I can't. Nothing." Her eyes held his. "What gives you the right to say I should allow my father in my son's life? I confided in you, Rick. You're a pastor, you owed it to me to tell me you knew my dad. Yet you waited. Why? Because you thought you could soften me up?" Head lifted high, Cassie glared at him. "Do you know how betrayed I feel? You've just confirmed that people, especially ministers, are not trustworthy." She walked away to join Laurel by the fire.

Rick stayed where he was. His heart ached as he replayed Cassie's words. She was right to feel betrayed.

It's my fault Cassie and her father are estranged. How can I make it up to her? To John?

Make it up to Cassie? How ridiculous. Rick was still withholding the truth. Not that John's finances were any of his business, except that it was his fault and he knew nothing he did could compensate for the damage he'd done.

Still. Cassie needed to shed the sorrow surrounding her past. She said she wanted to forget, but that wasn't possible with the soul-deep anger festering inside her. Like Noah, she needed to purge her resentment before she could move on. "Lord, please help her. Help me to help her." Rick offered the same prayer as he drove home. But questions had lodged in his heart, questions that demanded total honesty.

Am I so desperate to help Cassie so she'll regain her place in God's family, or because I feel guilty that her father neglected her for me? Or is something more at stake?

Cassie was like a bright light in his life. She gave him strength and support and the feeling that someone cared. And now he was addicted. He wanted to be her support, her bulwark, the one she could count on.

Okay, maybe he'd ruined what they'd begun

building, but he couldn't believe that. Because if he did, then he'd have nothing.

But his vow wasn't going away. He'd made it, he had a duty to be a man of his word, to honor his commitment. Rick struggled through the night. By morning he knew only one thing. He had to resist his personal feelings and step back from Cassie Crockett.

She was off-limits. But he couldn't just walk away from her needy heart.

The knot was too big for him to unravel. All Rick knew for sure was that God put him here to minister. For now he'd focus on his ministry to the Lives' boys, and Noah. Eventually, God would show him how to help Cassie.

Maybe He'd also show Rick how to ignore the feelings for her that were now rooted deep within his heart.

Chapter Five

In the three days that followed, Cassie spent every spare moment knitting scarves for Alicia, desperate to enrich her depleted savings. Then she'd start building an education fund for Noah.

As she sat at the kitchen counter, working on Alicia's scarf order, Rick's words tormented her. She couldn't wrap her mind around the fact that all those years when she'd thought her father had been avoiding her, he'd been helping homeless, parentless kids like Rick. She'd misjudged her father back then.

A tiny voice inside kept asking if she'd also misunderstood his words after Eric's death.

During her past two night shifts, Cassie had replayed her father's words over and over, desperate to understand their meaning.

You blame Eric. You blame God and the people who worship Him. You even blame me. Is it really us you can't forgive, Cassie? Or is it yourself?

Back then she'd been seething with resentment, certain he'd been hinting that she was at fault for Eric's mistake. Now, as she reexamined every memory, every event and every thought, Cassie was no longer so sure her interpretation had been right.

She had Rick to blame for her doubts, for putting the idea in her mind that she might have misjudged her father. She'd suffered the injustice of being wrongly judged. She could not tolerate the thought that she'd done the same thing to someone else, even her father.

She resented that Rick hadn't told her the truth earlier, but at least he had told her. Maybe she owed him an apology.

"Hi." Rick stood in the doorway to the kitchen, holding two stacked plastic containers in his hand.

"Hi." Cassie's heart gave its usual bump of excitement, betraying her as always. "What's up?" she asked, trying to quell it as she clicked her knitting needles together.

"Kyle told me Sara's doctor insists she gets off her feet more often so she has to cut back on baking." Rick's green-eyed gaze looked wary, as if she might lash out at him again. "I made a treat for the kids."

"That was nice of you." She strove to maintain perspective, desperate to keep this conversation from becoming personal, as so many others had. Rick Salinger already knew way too much about her. A little distance between them would be a good thing. "What did you make?"

"Devil's food chocolate cake." A smug look flickered across his handsome face.

"Is a minister supposed to be making devil's food?" she asked, tongue-in-cheek.

"I don't know if there are rules about cake. I didn't check." He set a large container on the table and revealed his masterpiece. "Four layers with double fudge frosting."

"Show-off." She chuckled at his obvious pride. "We'll be lucky if we don't *all* end up with diabetes after all that icing."

She recognized that he was hovering, trying to gauge her mood, so she nodded toward the coffeepot.

"Help yourself and have a seat."

"Thanks. Speaking of diabetes—how's Bryan?" Rick poured himself a cup of coffee, then sat across the table from her and thrust out his long legs. "Or do you and I need to initiate phase two?"

"What's phase two?" Cassie tilted her head to one side, curious even though she'd promised herself she would not be enticed by Rick's charisma.

"I don't know yet. I was waiting to see if we needed it before I came up with a plan." His wink and the smile slashing across his rugged face lent him a rakish look that crushed Cassie's resolve to keep her distance from Rick Salinger. "Maybe some kind of one-on-one intervention at my place that involves my lip-smacking elk burgers and sweet potato fries?"

"I had no idea you could get sweet potato fries up here."

"Churchill isn't exactly the end of the earth, you know." He chuckled at her raised eyebrow. "If you have the moolah, you can get anything. I don't have money, but I do have friends. One of them gave me some elk meat, and I brought a bag of sweet potatoes with me from Thompson a couple of trips ago."

"I thought people usually brought back clothes or books," Cassie teased. "You bring sweet potatoes?"

"Each of us has a secret vice. Mine is sweet potato fries." As he smiled at her, a silence fell between them, and Cassie wondered if he, too, was thinking about what had happened at the fireworks.

Rick leaned forward to peer into her eyes. "You're quiet. Are you worried about something?" He crossed his arms over his broad chest and waited. Cassie liked that he didn't try to rush her.

"Not exactly worried," she corrected. "More like confused."

"About?"

"My father." Cassie felt as if she was tiptoeing through a minefield as she tried to explain. "The other day you suggested I might have misunderstood what he said to me. I don't think I did, but—"

"But on the off chance you did—" He smiled. "You want to be sure, is that it?"

Cassie nodded. "I'm not exactly sure how to find out."

"I usually depend on God's leading," he said in a serious tone. "A little nudge of conviction deep inside often tells me when I need to right a wrong."

"I don't have any nudge of conviction. Certainly not from God," Cassie muttered almost, but not quite, beneath her breath.

"Don't you?" Rick's smile flashed again. "Isn't that exactly what your doubts are? When we begin to question something we thought was true, it's usually a sign that we need to seek God's guidance. Why don't you try doing that?" Steel-strong assurance laced his voice. She envied him that. "God doesn't let people down, Cassie. Not ever."

He let me down, she thought.

"Refusing to forgive is an acid that eats at you," he added very softly. "It hurts *you* most of all. If you can find a way to forgive, it allows your heart to heal." He paused, his gaze holding hers. "I'm sorry for not being honest, Cassie. I should have told you as soon as I remembered. I didn't because I wasn't sure how you'd take it and I was afraid you wouldn't want to be friends anymore."

Cassie didn't get a chance to respond. The boys burst into the house and ran into the kitchen, thrilled to find Rick sitting there. Cassie caught her breath at the pure delight that filled Rick's face when he saw them. How was it that this man who obviously loved kids didn't have any of his own?

Stop thinking about him. You can't trust him,

remember? Or maybe you can, but you shouldn't. You're not getting involved.

"Hey, guys." Rick grinned when, as one, the boys froze, almost drooling as they gaped at his chocolate confection sitting on the table.

Cassie laughed when Michael whispered, "Is that edible?"

Rick faked an indignant frown. "I'll have you know I baked that baby from scratch. With these hands." He extended his arms, as if to prove it.

Cassie sat back as he cut and proudly served his cake. Her awe at his thoughtfulness grew when he handed Bryan a plate with an individual chocolate cake.

"This is sugarless, Bryan," he murmured. "You can eat as much as you want."

"Hey, thanks, man." Bryan's face lit up. While the other boys bickered good-naturedly about who got the biggest slice, Bryan sat happily devouring his own private cake.

Cassie glanced at Rick and caught him studying her. She inclined her head toward Bryan and smiled. Rick nodded, but his gaze remained on her. Uncomfortable under that unblinking stare, Cassie grabbed the scarf she'd been making and worked while the kids bantered back and forth.

"Homework?" she asked when a pause in the conversation allowed.

"None. We had an assembly this afternoon," Rod answered. "We can play hockey until suppertime. Come on. Let's go, guys."

With a great deal of noise and shuffling, they cleared and loaded their dishes in the dishwasher, thanked Rick then hurried away. Noah left with them, but she noticed he hadn't said a word. That didn't bother her as much as the fact that he'd eaten only half his cake. She couldn't be sure, but she thought she saw him wince when Rod jostled his shoulder.

"Cassie, did you notice Noah?" Rick's green eyes grew dark with concern. "His shoulder?"

"I noticed." Seeing a mistake in the knitted row she'd just completed, she began tearing it out.

Rick sat down beside her. "What would you like to do?"

"I don't know." Cassie realized she was making a mess of her work so she set it aside. "Normally, Noah grumbles about every ache and pain, but he didn't say a word today."

"I'll try to sound out the other boys. Maybe they know what's up with him." He squeezed her shoulder. "Are you okay? Or maybe I should ask if *we're* okay."

Cassie looked up into his eyes, her stomach doing somersaults at his use of the word *we*. She nodded, knowing what he meant. "We are. It's all just confusing and complicated, and I'm not sure how to straighten everything out."

Rick rose. "Well, I'm sorry if I contributed to that confusion." Then, he gave her a heart-stopping smile and said, "Have some faith, Cassie."

Faith? she thought as he left. *Faith in what?*

She didn't trust God anymore. Faith in Rick? She wanted to trust him so badly. But she'd learned the hard way not to make herself vulnerable. So the only person she could have faith in was herself. And she had no answers.

With a heavy sigh, Cassie picked up the scarf-in-progress. As she began to work her needles, she realized that while Noah had left with the others, he hadn't gone outside with them—he was standing by the back door. She decided she'd try to have a private talk with him.

But when she went to him, he wouldn't let her get near. His face was ashen.

"Noah, what's wrong?"

"N-nothing." He stepped back, wincing when she touched him as if he were in pain.

"Honey, what's wrong with you?" she asked as her fears multiplied. "Talk to me."

"I t-think I have t-the flu. I'm going to m-my room." Without another word, Noah went inside his bedroom and closed the door.

He refused to talk to her the rest of that evening. Cassie had never felt more alone. Laurel was buried in government forms. Sara and Kyle had their own issues with the coming of their baby. The only person left to confide in was Rick. Her reactions to him disturbed her, but she had to ignore that because she had to do something about Noah. Someone had hurt, was hurting Noah and she had to put a stop to it.

Cassie inhaled deeply then picked up the phone. "Rick? I need help."

Ten minutes later she hung up with a sigh of relief. Surely Rick's offer of a meal of elk and sweet potato fries would make Noah open up.

Thank heaven for Rick.

"Come on in. Welcome."

The next evening Rick threw wide the door of his tiny cottage, shoved a box of old newspapers out of the way and stood back so Cassie and Noah could enter. "Sorry about that. I love reading the papers but I'm not faithful about getting them to the recycling center. You can lay your coats over that chair if you like. I don't have the luxury of a front hall closet."

"You certainly have the luxury of a fantastic view," Cassie said with a burst of enthusiasm. She quickly shed her outerwear, walked straight to the picture window overlooking the bay and peered out. "What are those things on the water?"

"Ice f-fishing h-huts," Noah stammered.

"He's right," Rick said with a smile. "They pull a hut onto the ice, cut a hole in the ice, drop a fishing line and then wait for a fish to bite."

"Really?" Cassie glanced at her son, surprised by his knowledge.

"The hut protects the fishermen from the wind. Some of them have heaters, too. There was a guy who even had a recliner in his. I call that fishing at a luxury level."

Rick could tell just by looking at Noah that he was probably going to have to carry the conversation this evening. That was fine—he was prepared for that. He'd prayed for the chance to reach Noah. This was that chance and he was grateful for it.

"Have a seat," he invited. "It will be a few minutes until dinner's ready."

"It smells wonderful." Cassie sat.

"Let's hope it tastes as good as you think it smells." Rick sat down next to Cassie, waiting to see what Noah would do. Noah then sprawled in Rick's favorite reading chair, no doubt attempting to create some distance. "So, how's it going, Noah? Managing to make friends at school?"

"I g-guess." Noah wouldn't look at them.

"I was talking to a friend of mine who teaches and he says the school is starting some self-defense lessons. Do you think you might be interested in that?" Rick asked, hoping to keep the evening light so the boy would relax and maybe open up.

Noah lifted his gaze. "I d-don't know," he muttered after a sideways glance at his mother.

"I studied it a few years ago. It's a good way to learn self-discipline."

Cassie was frowning, "I don't think—"

Rick saw Noah glare at her and nudged her.

"What do you think, Noah?" he asked.

"I might be interested," Noah said after a quick glance at Cassie.

"I'll let you know when the first meeting is and you can check it out for yourself, okay?" Rick waited for his nod. "I hear you guys are taking an evening field trip next week to see the Northern Lights from the viewing dome."

"Uh-huh." Noah's blue eyes shifted away.

"I might ask to tag along for that," Cassie said with a chuckle. "I've seen the lights at Lives, of course, but to watch from a viewing dome with someone explaining the flares would be really interesting."

"You're lucky you're here now." Rick leaned back.

"L-Lucky? Why?" Was that a flash of interest in Noah's eyes?

"January is the best month to see the Northern Lights. Fortunately, we've had unbelievably clear skies, thanks to that cold snap." Rick chuckled. "There's a blessing to everything."

Cassie's eyebrows lifted and she gave him a droll look just as the oven timer went off, breaking the silence.

"Dinner's ready." Rick led the way to the kitchen and seated Cassie and Noah. "I hope you enjoy it." He set a platter of his sweet potato fries on one trivet and the elk burgers on another, then pulled a plate of burger fixings from the fridge. "Shall we say grace?"

Both Cassie and Noah bowed their heads.

"Thank you, Father, for this food and these friends. Bless us now with Your presence, we ask in Jesus' name. Amen." Rick lifted his head and smiled. "Cassie, why don't you start the potatoes and Noah can start the meat."

As they ate, Rick kept the conversation light by asking Noah questions and inserting amusing anecdotes about his own youth on the street.

"It m-must have been n-nice to be your own b-boss." Noah tossed Cassie a glare.

"It might seem that way, but it was actually pretty difficult, Noah."

"Wh-what was s-so bad ab-bout it?" Noah demanded.

Rick chose his words carefully. "Maybe it was having to go through the garbage to find something to eat. Or trying to stay warm without getting arrested, or not being able to shower." He wanted Noah to realize what not having a home or a loving parent meant. "No, actually, I think not having anyone who cared about me was the worst of all. It's not a life I would ever want you to go through, Noah."

"How d-did you s-survive?" Noah leaned forward, his food forgotten. Rick could see that he'd gotten the boy's attention. He sensed that Cassie was sitting very still, practically holding her breath.

"People's generosity, church soup kitchens, shelters if they weren't too full." Rick shrugged. "I believe God protected me. I got into several situations where I could easily have died and didn't. I give thanks for His love every day."

Rick could feel Cassie's eyes on him but he focused on connecting with her son.

"Did you have gangs where you lived, Noah?" Rick studied the sullen boy.

"S-sure." Noah clearly didn't want to talk about it. "Can I h-have another b-burger? I n-never had elk b-before but it t-tastes really g-good."

"The secret is to cook it very slowly. Otherwise, it comes out tough as boots."

"I n-never ate th-that, either," Noah joked.

Rick chuckled as he shared an amused glance with Cassie. When was the last time they'd heard the boy make a joke?

When Noah scooped the rest of the fries onto his plate, Rick smiled and warned, "Leave some room for dessert."

"Wh-what is it?" Noah asked.

"Rice pudding." Rick almost laughed as disdain filled the boy's face.

"O-old p-people's f-food," he scoffed.

"Not the way I make it." Rick intercepted Cassie's reprimand by offering her the last burger. The last thing he wanted was for Noah to retreat back into his shell.

"It was all delicious, but I've had enough, thank you." She leaned back. "Where did you learn to cook, Rick?"

"I took lessons." He was used to the surprised stares.

"Man, c-cooking lessons?" Noah's face said it all—*wuss*.

"Remember, I never had a parent to teach me and

I like to eat," Rick said, meeting Noah's stare head-on. "Besides, women love a guy who can cook."

"D-doesn't look l-like it w-worked for y-you," Noah shot back after a quick survey of the house.

Cassie's face turned a deep shade of crimson, but she didn't say anything to Noah. Rick shrugged off the boy's comment, though the words hit a nerve deep inside.

"I don't think God has plans for me to marry," he said, finding himself avoiding Cassie's gaze. "Did your dad cook?"

"N-no. That was M-Mom's j-job." Belligerence glowed in Noah's blue eyes as he watched Rick remove their dinner plates.

"Lots of men think that way. But everyone should learn how to take care of himself, Noah," Rick said quietly. "That's the meaning of becoming an adult."

Noah's mouth pinched tight.

Lord, help me help them.

"What about when your mom was at work?" Rick asked.

Cassie opened her mouth to speak, but Rick gave the tiniest shake of his head. After a moment of indecision she gave in, but her expression warned that she would not allow Rick to continue to probe into their past.

"M-Mom had it r-ready for us." Noah glared at him.

Rick nodded, his suspicions about Cassie and Noah's past confirmed. Her husband hadn't been willing to do his share while she worked, and he'd taught Noah by example. As Rick set the bowls and spoons on the table, he noticed Noah absently rubbing his shoulder, as if it were still bothering him.

"Did you mind your mom going to work?" Rick asked.

"I d-dunno." Noah lifted his head just enough to shoot Cassie a dark look. "S-she worked a l-lot m-more after D-dad died."

"I had to, Noah," Cassie exclaimed. "We needed my salary to live on."

"It couldn't have been easy for either one of you." Rick set the steaming pudding beside his place. He served Cassie first, then a frowning Noah. "I'm sure your mom would have preferred to be home with you. Sometimes parents have to make hard choices."

Noah muttered something unintelligible as he accepted his dish with a turned-up nose. When he tentatively tasted his pudding, his eyes expanded. "Hey, it's g-good."

Rick burst out laughing. "You were expecting gruel?" he asked.

For the first time that evening, Noah smiled. "S-sort of," he admitted.

"It *is* delicious, Rick." Cassie smiled, but Rick noticed that the smile didn't reach her eyes.

"Thanks." He laughed when Noah scooped the last spoonful from his dish with gusto, then held out his bowl for a second helping. "Maybe Noah and I could make it at Lives one night." Noah shot him a dubious look. "It would save Sara from making dessert."

"Isn't th-that what she's p-paid for?" Noah asked.

"Noah!" Cassie's cheeks burned.

"Is that why you think Sara works at Lives?" Rick asked. "For the money?" He shook his head, deliberately keeping his voice light. "I'm pretty sure she could get two or three times her salary at a fancy hotel in Vancouver."

"Then wh-why doesn't s-she?"

"Because she loves the boys," Rick told him quietly. "Sara never had anyone to love or care about her when she was young. She doesn't want another kid to go through what she experienced. She wants everyone who comes to Lives to feel loved. That's why she spends so many hours coming up with delicious meals. Not because she *has* to," he emphasized. "Because she *wants* to."

Noah said nothing, but as the boy stared at the table, his second dish of pudding half-eaten, Rick could tell that what he'd said had made an impact. He shifted his gaze to Cassie and she nodded her approval.

"Well, if you're both finished, I guess it's time for cleanup." Rick winked at Cassie. "I have a rule in my house that women don't do dishes. So I guess it's up to you and me."

Noah jerked upright, his face full of dismay.

"Come on," Rick urged him. "Let's get started."

"Wh-where's the d-dishwasher?" Noah looked around the kitchen.

"Don't have one." Rick stacked their plates nonchalantly. "I do dishes by hand. Come on, dude. I've got a game ready, but we have to clean up this mess so we can use the table."

Noah stayed put until Cassie raised her eyebrows. He rose slowly, using his fingertips to carry the dirty dishes to the counter. Rick had to grin as Cassie turned away to hide her amusement.

"Don't worry about getting your hands dirty, son," he said in an avuncular tone. "They'll get really clean when you start washing."

He gibed, cajoled and teased Noah mercilessly, waiting for the boy to explode. But Noah didn't. He was angry, no doubt about that. But he stuffed down his emotions and soldiered on, which was the way he dealt with everything.

"Good job, Noah," he said as he removed the waterproof apron he'd tied around the boy's waist when they'd finished. "When Sara and Kyle come for a meal, Kyle refuses to wash dishes. He *claims* he has an allergy to dish soap."

"I th-think I d-do, too," Noah sputtered. He held out his reddened hands as proof.

"Nah," Rick said after a quick inspection. "That's just hot water. Really, thanks for your help, Noah. I hate doing dishes alone. Come on, let's play."

Noah didn't say anything, but he didn't look quite as miserable as he had. They played several rousing games and with each one Rick noticed that Noah seemed to shed more of the negativity that had clung to him since he'd first arrived.

"How about a drink before the next round?" Rick asked. "I could make some cocoa. I promise not to make you wash the cup, Noah."

Noah actually smiled, but his attention was on something else.

"N-no, thanks," Noah said. "C-could I l-look at those old b-books?" He motioned to a stack on the bookshelf in the farthest corner of the living room.

"You like old books?" Rick couldn't hide his surprise. He hadn't taken Noah-of-the-earbuds for the bookish type.

"I l-like h-history," Noah stuttered.

"Help yourself, then. Your mom and I will stay here and talk." Rick turned on the kettle then switched on his stereo. Soft hymns of praise filled the room. "Cocoa or coffee?" Rick asked Cassie.

"Cocoa's great." She had her knitting out. The needles clicked furiously.

By the time Rick set a big mug of cocoa in front of Cassie, Noah was sitting on the floor, swaying to the music, totally engrossed in the book he was reading.

"Thank you for doing this," Cassie murmured.

"I don't know if tonight has helped him much, but I've learned a few things." Cassie raised a questioning eyebrow so Rick continued, keeping his voice very soft. "He's suppressing a lot of anger—more than I had realized."

"I'm not sure I know what to do about it, though. He's still not ready to talk." Cassie's brown-eyed stare brimmed with doubt.

Trust, Rick wanted to urge her. *Trust God to help.* "As long as you keep talking to him, that should help." He sipped his cocoa, then decided to say what was in his heart. "It won't be an easy path, but God will be with you if you ask Him, Cassie. God's love isn't conditional. It's everlasting. No matter where you go, what you do, He will always love you. You can never escape God's love."

"You sound like my father." It was clear by her tone that she didn't mean this as a compliment.

"Have you figured out what to do about that yet?"

He could see that she hadn't in the tense rigidity of her shoulders He felt a little tense, too, knowing that he still hadn't told her the complete truth about his relationship with John.

"You keep saying God's love endures," she finally said, sounding very much like her angry son. "That we can't lose it."

"You can't." Rick couldn't stop himself from reaching out and brushing a wispy curl from her cheek with his forefinger. "Is that what you think, that you've lost God's love? Because you're wrong. God loves you, always has."

"Then why doesn't He show it?"

"Why do you think He hasn't, Cassie?" Rick's heart ached for the pain she kept built up inside. "He brought you away from your troubles, gave you several jobs here in Churchill. He gave you a wonderful friend in Laurel, and the chance to make more friends. God didn't abandon you, Cassie. He's right beside you."

Rick wanted to say more, to make her see how deep God's love for her was. But Noah stood at the end of the table, his face red and angry.

"What's wrong, Noah?" Cassie frowned.

"Wh-why do these b-books have my g-grandfather's name in th-them?" he demanded, thrusting out his hand with an old volume clutched in it.

Cassie looked at Rick in surprise.

"When I was living on the streets, your grandfather helped me, Noah. A lot." Rick said it evenly, meeting the boy's glare head-on. "Because of him I was able to finish school and college. Later he helped me get into seminary. Those books were his gift to me when I was ordained."

Rick knew he was in trouble before Cassie shot him a warning glance.

"You kn-new." Noah glared at Rick. "Y-you knew and y-you didn't t-tell us. Didn't you think you should tell us you knew my grandfather?"

"Noah, honey—" Cassie's voice died away as the truth dawned on Noah.

"I see." His gaze narrowed, his mouth tightened. "He already told you. I'm the only one who didn't know." His voice grew icy. "P-protecting m-me again, M-mom?" The scathing way he said it brought tears to Cassie's eyes.

"She didn't know about the books, Noah. *I'd* even forgotten how my collection of old books got started." Rick felt as if every inch of ground he'd gained with Noah was sliding out from under his feet. Worse than that, Cassie was now in trouble with her son, too.

"I w-want to l-leave." Noah dropped the offending book on the table, walked toward the door and grabbed his coat.

Cassie rose to her feet slowly. Her eyes met his and he knew exactly what her silent stare was asking.

Where's God now, Rick?

Chapter Six

For an entire week Cassie fretted over Noah. No matter how she examined her situation, she could not align it with Rick's assurance of God's love.

If God loved her so much, why didn't He help Noah?

But actually, maybe it wasn't God's fault. She probably should have told Noah that Rick had known his grandfather, especially because she knew how much Noah resented being kept out of the loop. He felt she treated him like a child.

She watched as Rick led the kids through their songs, savoring the familiar tunes. But she lost all sense of space and time when Noah began to sing in a pure, clear tenor tone.

He had his grandfather's sense of music. Her dad had always loved singing and for a moment she desperately wanted to hear his voice again.

"Still brooding over Noah?" Rick slid into the

pew where she'd sat to wait while the choir members cleaned up after practice.

"I'm not brooding," Cassie said defiantly, then sighed. "Maybe I am."

"I'm sorry." Rick touched her hand and Cassie felt that electricity she'd been working so hard to ignore. "What does Noah say?"

"He won't talk to me. He hardly speaks at all anymore because his stuttering is so bad. And this morning I noticed two new bruises." She swallowed the tears that threatened, hating that she'd become so desperate to confide her worries in Rick. "I think he's fighting. He did in Toronto. That's one of the reasons I decided to move."

"I wanted to talk to you about that." Rick's green pupils bored into her. "One of the choir kids hinted that Noah's being bullied."

"That's what I was afraid of. I'm sorry you're so deep in this with us, Rick," Cassie said and meant it. "Ordinarily I'd sound out Laurel, but she's busy trying to get another grant and I don't want to bother her with my problems."

"You can talk to me anytime, Cassie. You know that."

"Thanks." Cassie told herself not to feel special, that Rick gave that smile to everyone. But that did nothing to douse the warm glow inside. "I've had three conferences with Noah's teachers this week. Each of them expressed worry about his negative attitude. I don't know what to do anymore."

"Pray. Trust God to help you." Rick gave her a

sad smile. "I know what you're going to say, Cassie. You don't feel you can trust Him."

"No, I don't," she said.

"You're taking the view that bad things are God's fault because He doesn't stop them." Rick leaned forward to thank Bryan for gathering the choir's music.

Cassie couldn't help noting how unfailingly polite Rick was to everyone. He had an amazing rapport with a lot of Churchillians. Rick showed compassion and understanding, which made her feel terrible about being suspicious of his motives. And yet, she'd seen her father use his charm to co-erce his board into doing as he requested. And Eric had flaunted his early triumphs with the church's investments in order to get more from the congregation.

So, even though Cassie was impressed by Rick's interactions with the boys at Lives, she couldn't help suspecting that somehow, some way, he would use those triumphs to his own advantage. That's what the charismatic men she'd known had done. Guilt over her suspicions nagged her, but past experience was hard to shake.

She heard Rod call, "Snowball fight," and the rush of feet hurtling toward the door. Then all was quiet inside the church.

"Cassie?" Rick's hand pressed hers, drawing her attention back to the present, to the gentleness of his touch and his voice.

Somehow Rick only had to touch her, to reassure her, and her reservations about him flew from her mind. She had to be careful.

"Where did you go to just now?" He leaned forward, his focus totally on her.

"I was thinking about my father and Eric." And, because honesty was the best policy, she felt compelled to add, "and you."

"Me?" Confusion filled his expressive eyes. "Are you likening me to these men you don't seem to hold in very high esteem?" There was no amusement in the question.

"Not exactly. It's more that I see their actions more clearly now in hindsight," she said.

"And you think I'm like them." There was no anger evident in Rick's voice or his expression. He simply leaned back and waited for her explanation.

And that, Cassie decided, was the difference.

"I don't think you're like them at all. You don't work people."

"You mean I don't use them?" He raised one eyebrow, then smiled when she nodded. "Everyone has problems they're working through, everyone has reasons for their behavior that I can't possibly fathom. Everyone is doing the best they can to get through their lives." He shrugged. "It's my job as a pastor to help them on that journey, not to judge them."

"Does that apply to those who wrong you?" Cassie asked. As she waited for his answer, she was distracted by his good looks. His dark hair was a tousled mess. On someone else it would have looked unkempt but on Rick it added a mischievous quality and rendered him younger-looking than his thirty-one years.

"It applies to everyone, Cassie." Rick's dark eyes glowed as he spoke. "Yes, I get frustrated when people don't see my vision or accept my ideas. I'm human. But getting frustrated doesn't mean I expect them to give up their principles or objections."

"Why not?" His statement roused her curiosity.

"Because God shows Himself in different ways to different people. I have to keep my focus on showing God's love to people and leave the rest up to Him." Rick smiled. "And He does love us, Cassie. In Psalms it says He keeps an eye on us all the time. He remembers our prayers and He gathers our tears in a bottle. Those are the actions of someone who loves us dearly."

She mulled that over. But before she could pursue it, Michael burst into the sanctuary.

"Cassie, you have to come. Noah fell and hurt his arm."

Oh, God, her heart cried.

"He's sitting in the snow," Michael added as he raced beside her through the foyer. "When we try to help him up, he screams."

"He'll be okay, Cassie," Rick said, his quiet assurance filling her ear.

"Because God will help?" she demanded as she shoved open the door. "I should never have brought him to Churchill." Rick followed close behind. She saw Noah on the ground and her heart stopped. "It was a mistake."

"Or maybe God will turn this into a blessing," Rick murmured. Cassie ignored him and raced to her son.

"Where does it hurt?" she asked Noah, brushing a tender hand across his tousled hair.

"My arm. I think it's broken."

"I think so, too," Cassie murmured. "We have to get you to the hospital so they can set it. We'll help you stand, honey." She felt Rick move silently to help Noah stand and was overly conscious of his strong, supporting hand under her elbow, helping her into his car after they'd settled Noah. It would be so easy to lean on Rick. But his comment about Noah's injury being a blessing infuriated her. How could getting hurt be a blessing? She remained silent while Rick drove them to the medical center. Rick sat only inches away, but she couldn't speak to him.

To think that she'd been teetering on the edge of trusting.

Rick was wrong. God should have protected her boy. God's love had failed Noah.

But so had she.

"Noah?"

Rick watched as Cassie tentatively stepped into the treatment room after talking to the doctor, her face ashen. He followed her not because he had a right to be there, but because he very much wanted to help, to erase the vestiges of terror that he could still see in her eyes.

"I'm f-fine, M-mom. The d-doctor says I b-broke my a-arm." Noah moved his head when she reached out to smooth his hair.

"He also said you have a lot of bruises that have nothing to do with your broken arm. How did they happen, Noah?" Cassie sat on a chair next to the bed where he was perched.

"I keep slipping on the ice."

Cassie kept her intense gaze on his face. "You've become quite clumsy lately. Is that what you want me to believe?"

"Y-yes." He turned his head, shifting to gaze out the window.

"Look at me, Noah." Cassie waited for her son's attention.

Rick longed to beg her not to push the boy right now, but he saw her desperation and knew she needed answers. After hearing the doctor's concern about her son's bruised body, she had to be scared.

The boy turned his head and stared at his mother, but his blue eyes were devoid of emotion.

"Someone told Rick you're being bullied," she said in a quiet but anxious tone. "Is that true?"

"No." Noah didn't flinch, didn't move away, but neither did he embrace his mother when she sat beside him and slid an arm across his shoulders.

"You can tell me the truth," she murmured. "I just want to help you."

Cassie studied him for an interminable moment.

She finally drew her arm away when Noah refused to answer. Rick's heart hurt for her, knowing that she was reeling from the way her beloved son was shutting her out.

"Aunt Laurel is in the waiting room. She came as soon as she heard. Once your arm is set, we'll take you home." Cassie moved away and looked out the window. Rick could see the tears on her cheeks from where he stood.

The medical staff arrived and began to construct the cast that would immobilize Noah's arm.

"It's a fairly clean fracture," the doctor told Cassie. "Six weeks should do it." He turned to Noah. "This needs to heal so no roughhousing and no hockey. See me in a week to check on things. Got it?"

Noah nodded. The doctor asked Cassie to step outside again, and Rick grabbed his chance to be alone with the boy.

"You want to tell me what's really happening?" He stared into the pain-filled blue eyes. Noah shook his head once, firmly. "I might be able to help you."

Nothing.

"There are ways to handle bullying, Noah," he assured the boy quietly. "Ways that won't leave you vulnerable as the scapegoat for someone else. But the first step is to talk about it, to figure out what we're dealing with."

Noah's implacable stare told Rick he was wasting his time.

"Okay. But if you ever want help, you call and I'll be there. Deal?" He held out his hand.

Noah didn't shake Rick's hand. As his mother returned, he climbed off the table.

"S-see you l-later," he said. Then he walked through the door and headed toward the waiting room.

Laurel rushed over to them. "He's going back to school?"

"For now." Cassie sank onto a chair. "His whole body is a mess of bruises. The doctor says there are visible signs that Noah is being bullied." Cassie blinked furiously. "I have no idea what to do," she admitted, her voice broken.

"Pray," Laurel advised. "Sooner or later he'll open up."

Rick agreed about the praying part. Anger festered inside the boy and it was getting worse with every day that passed. But he couldn't say that to Cassie, wouldn't add to her anguish.

"I'll pray for him," he said, "and I'll try to get him to talk to me. Don't worry, we'll figure it out. Maybe you could arrange a phone call between Noah and his grandfather, Cassie."

"Why?" She glared at him.

"Because I believe he needs to talk to someone. He's mad at me for not telling him I knew your dad, and he doesn't seem to want to open up to you." Rick noted Cassie's wince and wished he'd phrased that better, but he pressed on. "Maybe if you spoke to your father, told him what's happening, maybe he'd get Noah to talk."

"I'll think about it," she murmured, her face troubled.

Rick wanted so badly to smooth away the worry. That's when he knew he was getting too involved with this little family—and for the wrong reasons. Was it God's love he wanted to demonstrate, or was it the need to take care of Cassie because of the feelings that continued to flourish inside his heart, despite his efforts to rout them?

Both. It was both.

It was time for him to distance himself from this impossible attraction for Cassie while figuring out a way to help her. He just wasn't sure his heart would survive the process.

"Noah could you stay after practice?" Rick asked.

Noah's lips tightened but he nodded. When they'd finished and the others were outside playing in the snow, Rick began his apology.

"I really am sorry I didn't tell you I knew your grandfather. I should have. He was a very important man in my young life. I honestly did forget about the books, though."

Noah studied him for a long time then finally shrugged. "Doesn't matter."

"Sure it does. Your grandfather is obviously an important person to you. I should have said something." Rick waited, praying. *Please let him talk. Please.*

"He's the only one who's honest with me," Noah muttered.

Aghast, Rick couldn't hide his astonishment.

"You don't think your mom's been honest with you?" he asked.

Noah held his gaze for several moments. Then he looked away.

"I didn't say that," he said. He rose. "I need to go. They're waiting for me."

Rick placed his hand on the boy's good arm and waited until he had his entire attention.

"Just for the record, Noah. I will always be honest with you."

"Sure." Noah left.

Rick sat on a pew and tried to figure out the meaning of what he'd just heard. He'd keep working on Noah, find out more. Then he'd talk to Cassie.

Rick paused on the threshold of the family room at Lives, watching as Cassie knelt beside one of the boys in the throes of an epileptic seizure.

"Relax, Michael," she murmured in a reassuring tone.

"Anything I can do?" Rick asked.

She looked up, startled, glanced at him and shook her head.

In the week since Noah's incident Rick had been visiting Lives Under Construction a lot. He'd specifically chosen times when he knew Cassie had a shift at the hospital so he could meet up with Noah. But now, seeing her pretty face, his heart took up the familiar double-time rhythm in his chest, forcing him to realize he'd had little success in quelling his responses to her, but at least he'd found a tiny crack in Noah's armor.

"He's coming out of it now." After checking her watch, Cassie noted the time in a little booklet she had in her pocket. Worry clouded her eyes, but the loving touch of her ministering hands continued.

Rick knelt opposite Cassie to clasp Michael's hand in his. She tossed him a brief smile.

"Lie still for a moment and get your bearings," she urged as Michael's eyelids fluttered.

Michael's amber eyes slowly opened. He stared at her, misery and shame swirling in his gaze.

"It was worse this time, wasn't it?" he asked in a slightly slurred tone.

"A little longer," she agreed.

"I wish it would just kill me." Grimacing, he accepted Rick's hand to help sit up.

"Don't say that, Michael," Cassie said. "These attacks will diminish eventually. The doctors told you that."

"Yeah, but when?" He touched his temple gingerly. "I think I hit myself."

"You knocked against the table before I could catch you," Cassie explained. "I'm sorry."

"It's not your fault." Michael's voice carried a

return of the depression Rick had heard in several previous visits.

"Do you feel like getting up, maybe moving to the sofa? It might be more comfortable." Cassie smiled her thanks at Rick when he helped the boy stand upright.

Michael's feeble grip fell away as he lowered himself onto the couch. "Is it a sin to want to die, Rick?"

"Well, I don't think God appreciates us rejecting His gift of life," Rick temporized, his radar going into full alert at the question.

"I think dying is the only way I'll ever be free of these seizures," Michael murmured.

"That's not true," Cassie countered.

But Rick heard the reservation in her tone. He watched as she draped a damp cloth on Michael's brow and smoothed his hair. He'd seen Cassie's devotion to her patients before, but this was more than a nurse doing her job. This was Cassie's motherly heart enfolding a troubled kid.

"Can I tell you something, Michael?" Rick sat down across from the prone boy, shifting so Michael could see his face without altering his position.

Cassie sat down near Michael, as well, intently observing him. Rick inhaled then spoke the words God had laid on his heart.

"You're not here by accident, Michael. You're here because God has plans for you. Good plans."

"How do you know?" Michael shifted a little higher on his pillows, his interest clear.

"It's in the Bible. There's a verse where God says He knows the plans He has for you, plans for good and not for evil, plans to give you a future and a hope." Rick smiled.

Michael visibly struggled to adjust his thinking.

"Maybe it's hard to see now, but God has good things in store for you," he said, feeling the intensity of Cassie's stare. "What you have to do is be ready for them."

"How? I can't stop the seizures." The hope that had flickered in Michael's eyes sputtered out. "None of the doctors can tell me if they'll stop for sure. What hope is there in that?"

"The hope isn't in the situation, Michael. The hope is in God. You trust Him to keep His promise to help you." When Cassie checked Michael's pulse again, Rick rose. "We can talk again whenever you want. But I think Cassie would like you to rest now."

"Yes, I would." She took the damp cloth from Michael's forehead. "Rest for a while. Think about something nice."

"Like my saxophone," he murmured in a drowsy tone.

Cassie beckoned to Rick to follow her out of the room, closing the door gently. Once they were in the hall, she said, "I did ask him if he knew where his saxophone was, after you suggested it. He told me his parents sold it to punish him."

Rick shook his head in dismay as they walked toward the kitchen.

"Thanks for your help. Michael seemed to relax after you quoted that passage from Jeremiah. It used to be a favorite of mine, too."

"Not anymore?" He noted the yawn she couldn't quite smother.

"Oh, I still think it's a great verse." She poured herself a second cup of coffee.

"Just not for you. Right?"

"Something like that." She lifted a hand to rub the back of her neck.

"You're tired."

"I was up with Daniel last night." She sighed. "He's still struggling with withdrawal so he has nightmares. I try to be there when they get too intense."

"You care a lot about these boys, don't you?" Rick didn't have to ask. He already knew the truth, saw it in the tenderness of her gaze whenever it rested on one of the boys. He also saw that the burden of caring for them was wearing her down. "You need a break. Get on some warm clothes."

"Why?" She blinked at him in surprise.

"We're going snowshoeing."

"I don't know how to snowshoe," Cassie sputtered. "Besides, I have to keep an eye on Michael."

"I'm sure Laurel will be happy to check on him while you're out. Any other excuses?" He grinned when her mouth opened and closed several times.

"I didn't think so. All work and no play makes Jack a dull boy, but it does the same thing for Jill."

"Something you learned in medical school?" Cassie gibed.

"Seminary." He chuckled when she rolled her eyes. "Well?"

"Truthfully? I'd love to get some fresh air. I'll check with Laurel and see if it's okay with her. I'll change and be right back." She hurried to the door, paused then turned. "You're sure you have time?"

"Positive," Rick said, ignoring his better judgment, which told him that this wasn't the way to create distance. "I'll get my gear out of the car."

Kyle was waiting for him when he returned. "I didn't realize you were here. Were you looking for me?"

"Actually, yes." Rick felt his face heat up when Cassie appeared and Kyle took a moment to look back and forth between them. "Michael had another seizure. He's resting now so I suggested Cassie take a break and go snowshoeing with me. Can she borrow your snowshoes?"

Kyle raised an eyebrow but all he said was, "Sure. They're inside the shed. Have fun."

"Thanks." Rick zipped up his suit and grabbed his gloves, grateful that his friend hadn't demanded an explanation right then and there—because he didn't have one.

He checked that Cassie was ready to go. "Okay?"

She nodded.

The early afternoon sun blazed on the white

snow, almost blinding in its intensity. Rick helped Cassie strap on Kyle's snowshoes then donned his own. Cassie caught on quickly and soon they were tramping over the tundra, their breath forming white clouds around them.

"You're good at this," he complimented.

"It's actually a lot of fun," she puffed, pausing to gaze around. "I've wanted to get out and explore but haven't had much time. Oh, look." A rabbit scurried across the snow, barely visible as he blended into his surroundings.

"There's a small creek over there," Rick told her. "Not that it will be running in this weather, but that thicket makes a good hiding place for animals. Want to take a look?"

Cassie nodded and set off at a quick clip. Rick followed, admiring the way her blond curls framed her face. Cassie was truly beautiful. There was no denying it.

Rick quickly checked the direction of those thoughts. This was an outing to have fun. That's all.

Something cold and wet smacked him on the side of his head.

"Hey!"

"I thought maybe you'd fallen asleep," Cassie teased, her laughter echoing across the barren land. "How come you slowed down?"

"I got caught admiring the view," he muttered as he scraped snow from his collar.

"What did you say?" She tipped her head to one

side like a curious bird, the pure angles of her face lit by the sun.

"Nothing." Rick forced his mind to clear. In several quick strides he was beside her. "You want a snowball fight? I can give you a snowball fight." He bent to scoop up a handful of snow and rolled it menacingly between his hands.

"No, no!" she yelped, turning awkwardly to race across the snowpack as quickly as she could. "I was just teasing!"

Rick followed, took aim and threw. The snowball landed on the top of her green hood. Without pause he made a second missile and hit her in the back. Cassie's laughter echoed through the afternoon but soon her speed tripped her up and she landed with a whoosh in the snow.

Rick plowed toward her, forming another snowball as he moved. When he reached her, he loomed over her. "Prepare to have your face washed."

"I'll freeze," she protested, still chuckling. When he leaned down, she squealed, but in an about-face of courage, tipped her head so she was looking directly at him. "Okay, I'll take my punishment."

Rick was instantly caught up in her brown eyes, in the way her curls kissed her cheeks and the proud thrust of her chin, daring him. Finally he tossed the snowball over her head then held out a hand.

"Come on. If your racket hasn't chased away every animal within ten miles, we might still see something."

Cassie's laughter died as she studied him. Then she held out her mittened hand and let him pull her upright. Cassie's snowshoes got tangled in his and she lost her balance, tumbling against him, her hands pressed against his chest.

Her brown eyes, huge now, met and held his. "Sorry."

Rick's arms automatically went around her. He couldn't speak, couldn't move, couldn't tear his gaze from her. His heart threatened to pound through his chest. He felt certain Cassie could hear it, but all he could do was stand there, stunned by the strength of his urge to kiss her, to touch his lips to her soft mouth. He leaned forward just the tiniest bit.

"R-rick?" Her voice emerged in a breathy gasp. Seconds passed and he didn't release her. At last, she dropped her hands from his chest and stepped back, untangling her snowshoes from his. "I thought we were going to see some animals," she murmured.

"We are." Rick exhaled. "Race you."

He wheeled away and marched across the snow in giant strides, surging toward the thicket, inhaling deeply as he moved, trying to cleanse his heart and mind of Cassie. He glanced back once. She was standing where he'd left her, studying him.

Determined to regain control, Rick faced forward and kept going until he reached the tree stump where he often sat and watched the animals. He filled his lungs and forced his heart to slow down. By the time Cassie arrived, he had regained his composure. He even managed to give her a friendly smile, as if he'd totally dismissed the intimate moment they'd shared.

"Have a seat." He swiped the snow off another stump and patted it. "It's not the most comfortable, but it's the best view."

"It's pretty here. It looks like a Christmas wonderland." Cassie, too, seemed determined to ignore those few awkward minutes. She sat down next to him, her shoulder brushing his.

A short while later a white-coated Arctic fox appeared not thirty feet away. Cassie made no sound, though when the fox came within several feet of them, her hand slid into his.

"It's okay," Rick reassured her in a low murmur. "She's checking us out. She probably has a den with kits in it nearby. Try not to move."

He sat beside Cassie, too aware of her so close to him. He felt every motion she made, heard her swift intake of breath when the mother fox carried one of her babies into the snow for a quick wash, then hurried it back inside when a dark shadow circled overhead.

"She won't come out for a while now," he explained. "She knows there's danger."

Several moments passed before Cassie's hand slid out of his. "We've been gone awhile," she said checking her watch. "I should get back and check on Michael."

"Okay." Rick rose, sad that their few moments

alone together were over but also somehow relieved that they'd soon be with other people. He needed to get his thoughts in order, to remember the vows he'd made to God and to focus on God's priorities.

He pushed through the snow in silence, following the trail their earlier tracks had made. He focused on what he saw. Frosted crests of snow peaked among wild grasses that had pushed through wind-polished hillocks of white.

"It's very serene, isn't it?" she said in a hushed voice.

"Yes." Rick wished he felt that serenity inside. Instead, he felt off-kilter and confused. He waited until they were almost back to Lives, then he turned to face Cassie.

"Is something wrong?" Cassie asked, a question on her face.

Rick had been going to say something about the two of them, but suddenly he couldn't find the words. Anyway, he didn't want to break the connection he'd felt. Not yet.

"I wanted to ask about Noah," he said instead. "I'm guessing you haven't made much progress?" He waited for the shake of her head. "He's been very quiet at choir, too. I thought he might stop coming, but he hasn't."

"I'm glad."

"Me, too. He seems to enjoy singing," Rick murmured. "I wish I could give him more attention, but I have my hands full with directing the boys and accompanying them on guitar."

"I thought Lucy was playing piano." Cassie undid her snowshoes.

"The arthritis in her hands makes it too difficult for her. Playing on Sundays is the most she can manage." Rick met her gaze when she looked up at him, but he had to look away. Those few moments in the snow kept intruding.

"I suppose I could help, if I'm not called in for a shift," Cassie offered hesitantly.

"We'll gladly take any and all help," he said. "What would you like to do?"

Cassie looked at him as if he'd grown two heads.

"Play," she said. "I thought you wanted a pianist."

"You play the piano?" He grinned. "I wish I'd known that a couple of weeks ago."

"The only thing is, I wonder how Noah will react," she said. "What if my being there makes his stuttering worse?"

"That won't be an issue," Rick assured her as he stepped out of his snowshoes. "Noah doesn't stutter when he sings."

"At all? I mean he didn't the day I was there, but I thought that was an exception." Cassie's face lit up.

"His voice doesn't falter on a single note."

"Maybe this is one area where he could shine," Cassie said.

"That's what I'm thinking." Rick walked with her toward the house.

"Can I ask you something?" Cassie pulled her hands from her mitts and blew on them to warm them.

"Anything. My life is an open book." Curious to hear her question, he waited.

"Why do you spend so much time at Lives? Are you hoping your work here will help you get a promotion to a better church?"

Rick bristled at the insinuation he thought he heard in Cassie's words, then decided her question was legitimate, given her past history with those who'd called themselves Christians. He looked into her eyes and spoke from his heart.

"I'm not interested in padding my bio, Cassie. I try to help wherever I can because that's what I promised God I'd do." He shook his head at the cascading memories. "I've made a lot of mistakes, hurt a lot of people. If one kid avoids the same mistakes and the repercussions because of me, then maybe I'll have repaid a bit of the debt I owe God."

She studied him for a long time, her gaze searching, questioning. Finally, she nodded and led the way inside.

As Rick followed, an inner voice reminded him he'd also promised God that he would give up his yearning for love and a family of his own. And yet, every day he was getting more entangled with lovely Cassie Crockett and her son.

Worse than that, Rick still hadn't been completely honest about his past with her father. He hadn't told her that he was the reason her father hadn't been in a position to offer her any financial help when Eric died.

For a moment, the thought of everything Rick had cost Cassie and Noah was almost more than he could bear.

Chapter Seven

The whirling snowstorm outdoors matched the blizzard of confusion inside Cassie's soul. This crazy attraction to Rick Salinger muddled her thinking. One moment she could hardly wait to see him, the next she was desperate to avoid him.

"Mom? C-can we h-have some m-more p-popcorn, p-please?" Noah held out the massive bowl she'd filled only a few moments ago. At least, that's what it seemed like.

"Sure. Why don't you make it?" She watched as he measured oil and popcorn kernels, then slid the pot back and forth over the stove. The mouthwatering aroma of warm popcorn quickly filled the room. "Are you okay?" she asked, wishing he'd talk to her.

"I'm s-sick of this s-stupid cast." Noah flicked off the switch on the stove, but couldn't lift the pot to empty it. He stood back while Cassie did that. "I wonder if Rick will cancel."

"Cancel?" She frowned. "Cancel what?" After two consecutive night shifts at the hospital, her mind felt jumbled as her body took its time readjusting to regular hours.

"He s-said he was g-going to come t-tonight, with h-his guitar, so we c-could have a s-sing-along." Noah peered out the window. "Maybe h-he won't make i-it in this."

"Do you like singing?" She pretended nonchalance, nibbling on a handful of popcorn while Noah melted butter.

"Yeah. The c-choir is g-great." Noah's face beamed with enthusiasm. Cassie was astounded. She couldn't remember the last time she'd seen him look so happy.

"Rick asked me to accompany the choir because Lucy's struggling with the music. Will that bother you?" Cassie asked.

"Nah. Mrs. Clow m-makes lots of m-mistakes." In the midst of pouring melted butter over the popcorn, Noah's head lifted. "What's th-that?" He dropped the butter dish and raced toward a window. "It's R-Rick and s-someone else," he said. "Mr. S-Stonechild, I th-think. They're r-riding a s-snowmobile."

Cassie heard Laurel going to the door and hid a smile as she imagined her friend's reaction to seeing Teddy Stonechild again. The couple never seemed to hit it off, though they snuck looks at each other whenever they were in the same room.

Cassie wondered if, in spite of their bickering, they were secretly attracted to each other.

Rick's voice echoed down the hallway.

There it went again, her silly thumping heart almost pounding out of her chest. Cassie was tempted to rush upstairs in an attempt to avoid him, but that would be childish.

Besides, she wanted to see him again.

"You keeping this popcorn for yourself?" Rick asked from behind her, laughter in his deep rich tone.

"That's Noah's. You'll have to ask him." Her skin prickled at his nearness but she turned and faced him, anyway, hoping her face didn't give her away.

"Can I share your popcorn, Noah?" Rick grinned.

"S-sure." Noah's face lost its bored expression as he handed Rick a bowl.

"Thanks." Rick served himself fully one-third of the popcorn they'd just made. He winked at Cassie over his shoulder. "I like the buttered stuff best."

"So do I." Noah stared at the mostly unbuttered remains.

"I'll melt more," Cassie told him, going to the stove. "Rick, I'm surprised you got here in this storm."

"This isn't a storm. This is a little dustup." He laughed out loud. "At least that's Teddy's take. The man is fearless."

"W-was it f-fun, coming h-here?" Noah asked.

Cassie glanced at Rick. She didn't want Rick to encourage her son to take risks.

Noah, she suddenly realized, was beginning to look up to Rick. Too much?

Rick's green eyes locked with hers in understanding. Then he turned to Noah.

"Not exactly fun, Noah," he said in a sober tone. "But we're both fairly experienced on this terrain and we always note our landmarks. I'm not sure we'll be able to go back tonight, though. The wind has kicked up a lot since we left."

"You could have canceled," she said.

"I promised the kids I'd be here and I keep my promises." Time seemed to freeze as Rick's gaze clung to hers.

In a flash Cassie recalled every instant of those moments in the snow when his arms had wrapped around her and she'd felt his heart race. His green-eyed stare told her he'd been as affected by the encounter as she had. While that flattered her ego, it also terrified her. She didn't want to be under the influence of attraction. Not ever again.

"Mom, you're g-going to burn the b-butter."

She blinked and found Noah staring at her. "Sorry. Here," she said, pouring it on his popcorn.

"Your mom is probably tired from her hospital shifts," Rick said. "Why don't we invite her to join us in singing."

"N-no w-way." Noah shook his head vehemently.

"Why not?" Rick frowned, clearly bothered by

his abrupt refusal. "Your mom deserves to have some fun. She works hard and—"

"She c-can't s-sing," Noah told him. "Th-they even k-kicked her off the ch-church choir."

"Noah!" Cassie's cheeks burned. She was totally embarrassed by Rick's laughter. "Let's hear if you do better," she snapped before scooping up the bowl of popcorn and going into the big family room.

"Noah, my man, you have to be more careful about the lady's feelings," Rick whispered just loud enough for her to hear.

Cassie ignored their smothered laughter and handed the bowl to Michael. "Help yourself," she ordered, "and pass it to the others. Rick's already eaten his share and Noah doesn't want anymore."

"Hey!" Noah protested. "N-not t-true."

Cassie was glad for the clamor that followed Rick's entrance. While the boys high-fived him, she sat in a corner chair and waited for her face to cool off. But she couldn't keep her eyes off the handsome preacher, especially when he pulled out the ukulele he'd brought in his backpack and began coaxing music from it.

How could one man be so blessed? Rick had good looks, the most gentle, giving spirit she'd ever known and an unbelievable ability to play and sing.

Sometimes, Cassie decided, life was not fair. How was she supposed to stay away from a man like Rick?

As the boys sat in a circle around Rick, Cassie

could only watch, astounded by the way he used his musical gift to reach each boy. Most of them hadn't sung before but Laurel had coaxed them to join the choir. Now they didn't even suspect Rick was teaching them harmony as he guided them through a series of choruses, encouraging one boy to take the lead line here and another there. Even the most reluctant couldn't help joining in on the fun.

Now, for the first time, Cassie was truly grateful her parents had insisted she take piano lessons. Those years of lessons gave her the ability to realize the extent of Rick's talent. This was a man whose music poured from his heart and his soul.

Rick even managed to draw Laurel and Teddy into the singing. Without pause he adapted and arranged songs to suit everyone. Watching him, understanding flooded her. Rick's ability to engage everyone around him lay in his openness with them. He accepted everyone as they were—warts and all. Despite opposition, he kept right on doing what he thought was right. Cassie envied him that quality—especially because she didn't have it.

Was that why Noah admired him so much? Because Rick was strong and focused? Was that why she admired Rick? Because his faith didn't wobble as hers did? Because he knew what he believed and he trusted God no matter what?

It wasn't that she didn't want to trust God. But— there was always that "but" of fear that He'd abandon her. That's what she couldn't shake.

"It's getting late, guys. I think Laurel would like

us to conclude our sing-along." Rick strummed a slower, quieter tune. "How about if we sing this one like a prayer of thanks to God for giving us His son as a token of His great love for us."

He played the first chord. As one, the boys' voices rose in a sweet offering of praise. Cassie's heart cracked as the young voices soared and filled the room. She'd once been like that, devoted to God, determined to serve Him no matter what.

Rick caught her eye and smiled. His face shone as his voice blended with the boys' in a mellow tenor. Sometimes he dipped into harmony. At others his voice spiraled with the melody, worshipping. His eyes closed as the last voice died away into hushed silence until nothing but the whine of the wind outside was audible.

"Thank You, God, for these boys, for Lives Under Construction and for Your love. We ask you for a restful sleep and bright hope for tomorrow. In Jesus' name. Amen." Rick opened his eyes and smiled at each boy. "Good night, guys."

The reverence of the evening seemed to linger as the boys expressed their thanks then filed out. Laurel hurried to find quilts for Teddy and Rick, claiming there was no way they could get back to town with the almost whiteout conditions that now whirled outside. Teddy left to check that everything was okay outside, leaving Cassie alone with Rick.

"I never fully appreciated what an amazing talent you have," she said sincerely.

"It's a sweet time with God when hearts are in

harmony." He put away his ukulele then sat down beside her and studied her. "You look pensive."

Cassie studied the lean lines of his face, the heart-stopping splendor of his emerald eyes and the way his smile revealed his inner joy. She decided this wasn't the moment.

"Come on, Cassie. You can tell me anything. I'm a minister, remember? I've heard it all." His hand closed around hers and gave it a squeeze. "What's wrong?"

"I'm concerned about Noah," she said, easing her hand from his as she tried to quell the tremors his touch aroused.

"We all are," he agreed.

"This is something different. Something to do with you." With Rick studying her so intently, Cassie hated saying the words, but the facts hadn't changed. "Noah's getting very attached to you. His face when he realized you'd arrived—" She gulped, shook her head. "I don't want him hurt, Rick."

"I'm not going to hurt Noah, Cassie." Rick looked stunned as he said the words, as if what she was concerned about was a complete impossibility.

"You won't be able to help it," she shot back, angry that her tears were so near the surface. "You'll leave, move on to something better, as you should. You have your life to live. But Noah." She stopped, swallowed, then continued. "I believe Noah will be devastated when you go."

"I'm not leaving, Cassie," Rick insisted.

"Not yet," she responded.

"Well, I won't say not ever because none of us knows the future. But as far as I know, I am staying here in Churchill." He ducked his head so he could peer into her eyes. "Is this wishful thinking on your part?"

There was a hint of humor in his question but Cassie ignored it. She was deadly serious. "Noah's beginning to look up to you, Rick. He talks about what you say all the time. I can hear in his voice that he's starting to admire you as he hasn't admired anyone since—"

"Eric. Who left him. I get it, Cassie. But I am not his father and I don't abandon people." Rick's forehead furrowed suddenly. "Is this your way of asking me to back off from trying to help Noah?"

"No!" She shook her head, surprised by how little she wanted Rick to leave them alone. "Noah needs you in his life."

She needed to make him understand. "It's just that working here, seeing the problems these boys have as a result of dysfunctional homes, has made me even more aware of my responsibility to Noah and of how quickly he could become attached to you."

Rick's hand covered hers, warm and protective. "You're a great mother, Cassie. I promise I'm not just going to disappear on Noah. You have my word."

"Thank you." Cassie swallowed. She wanted to trust him, wanted to believe in him so badly. But vestiges of the past held her like chains.

"You have to trust someone sometime, Cassie. Trust me. I won't let you down."

She opened her mouth to respond but a loud wail, followed by Noah's bellow, interrupted.

"M-mom! It's M-Michael!"

Cassie rose and raced out of the room. Michael was on the floor of the room he shared with Noah, his body contorted in a grand mal seizure. Her heart sank at the realization that this seizure was far stronger than any Michael had suffered before. She grabbed a washcloth off a nearby chair, rolled it up and placed it between his teeth to protect his tongue, then turned his head to one side. When she realized Rick was behind her, she motioned him to kneel by the boy's head.

"Stay here and keep him from hurting himself. I have to get his anticonvulsant." She ran down the hall to her medicine cabinet, loaded a syringe and hurried back. Kneeling, she plunged the needle in, but Michael didn't seem to respond. "Rick, get Laurel."

"I'm here," her friend said. "What do you need?"

"Alert the air ambulance. I want Michael airlifted out to Winnipeg." Cassie grabbed a blanket from the bed and draped it over him to keep him warm. "He needs to see a specialist as soon as possible. Make sure they know they need a nurse on board. If they can't get anyone, I'll go with him."

Laurel nodded and hurried away. Cassie looked at Rick.

"Tell me what you need," he said. His eyes met hers.

"Will you take Noah out of here and get him set up in a different room for tonight?"

Rick touched her shoulder. "Don't worry about anything else, Cassie. Just help Michael."

"I don't think I can do any more for him," she murmured sadly.

"God can. Trust Him, Cassie. I'll be right back." Rick squeezed her hand then left, closing the door behind him.

Trust God. Dare she? What if He failed her?

Cassie wavered, but in the end she was too afraid to trust Him so she concentrated on Michael, noting every change as he began to regain consciousness. Over and over she uttered words of encouragement, assuring him that he was safe in his room at Lives, willing him to come out of it.

"You had a seizure, Michael. But it's okay. You're okay." The seizure slackened so she removed the cloth from his mouth. "I'm here, Michael."

Finally he began to rouse, eyelids flickering until at last, he opened his eyes and peered up at her. Cassie checked his pupils and his pulse before she heaved a sigh of relief. He was okay for now. But what about in the future? The seizures were getting longer and more intense. Where was God's love for this poor boy?

"Relax now. Sleep if you want. You're okay," she repeated over and over.

A few moments later Michael drifted to sleep. Cassie took his vitals several times more, watching as slowly—too slowly—they returned to normal.

"Everything okay?" Rick whispered.

"For now. Can you stay with him for a few minutes? I have to call his doctor."

"Sure. Should I move him to the bed?"

"No. Leave him here for now. I don't want to disturb him."

When Rick held out his hand to help her up she took it, glad to rely on his strength. She didn't expect it when he pulled her into his arms and drew her close.

"Cassie. Take a breath. Lean on me."

Lean on him? Dare she allow herself that luxury? But it felt right to lean her head on his shoulder, to let him smooth his hands over her shoulders and ease the stress there.

"Michael's going to be fine." Rick's voice held such confidence, such peace that Cassie couldn't argue. It was enough to smell the musky spice of his aftershave, to relax her guard, if only for a minute, and let someone else take over. "God's in control."

"How can you be so sure?" she whispered. It felt so right to rest in Rick's arms.

"Because I trust Him and because I know He

cares for Michael far more than any human ever could." Rick stroked her back and shoulders as he spoke, soothing her.

Suddenly Cassie realized that she was too close to this man, too needy, too dependent. When she was in his arms, she wanted things she couldn't have. She was afraid to trust him. She eased out of his embrace, the loss of his arms around her like a physical pain. "I need to go."

"I know." Before he let his arms drop away, Rick pressed a kiss against her forehead. "You're an amazing woman, Cassie Crockett. God has blessed you with a wonderful talent for caring for those who hurt."

"God has?" she asked, irritated by the comment.

"Yes, God." Rick stepped back, smiled and touched his forefinger to her cheek. "That sense of compassion that's embedded so deeply inside you is straight from God. He's gifted you with the empathy to see a needy heart or a hurting body and help. Let go and let Him work through you."

Cassie left the room to make her phone call with Rick's words ringing in her ears. Let God work through her? It was a prayer she'd prayed throughout her teen years—to be used by God. Instead, she felt used by her husband and her father. Was she now finally where God intended her to be— alone and broke, with a son in emotional trouble?

And falling for a man who deserved to be trusted and loved—two things she was no longer sure she could do?

* * *

Rick lay sleepless on Noah's bed, thinking of Cassie and all she'd done tonight. She was a woman beyond compare.

Michael's rhythmic breathing filled the room.

Thank you, Lord, for being with this boy. Please help me help him overcome the depression that is upon him.

There were so many needs in this building, so many hearts that needed the Master's mending. Rick spent the next hour praying for each one.

When he was finished, he thought about jobs he needed to do at the church, office work that had waited too long, visits he'd been meaning to pay.

But no matter how he tried to avoid it, his thoughts always returned to those precious few moments when he'd held Cassie in his arms.

The sweetness of her, the love she showered on kids society wanted punished—that stuck with him. She really loved these troubled kids. She was an awesome mother.

Rick replayed the years he'd struggled to live on the streets and imagined how different it would have been had Cassie been there. What would it be like to have her to lean on when his job overwhelmed him and he felt unable to comfort another soul? What would it be like to let her comfort him?

He felt dazed by his thoughts. He was beginning to care for her. He wanted to help her through the tough times and the good. He wanted to be able to run to her when life overwhelmed.

But that couldn't be.

He couldn't care for Cassie Crockett. Not if he was going to keep his vow to God.

The joy he'd known leeched away. Love, companionship, a family—that wasn't for him. God didn't want that for him.

Then he remembered her earlier question about leaving. Was that what God was telling him, that he should leave here if that was the only way he could keep his vow?

The thought of leaving this place he loved, of walking away from the woman who made him yearn to fulfill his dreams, filled Rick with pain.

"Please don't make me," he whispered.

But what choice did he have? If he couldn't control these feelings for Cassie, if he couldn't figure out how to keep his vow without losing her, then leaving might be his only choice.

The rest of the night passed in a tug-of-war as Rick fought to suppress his feelings. He begged God to take away his tender feelings for her. Just before dawn he finally gave in and asked God for a new mission, a place to go where he would not be tempted to break his vow to serve God alone.

He'd promised Cassie he wasn't leaving. He'd repeated that promise to her and he'd meant it. The thought of breaking that promise filled him with pain. But what choice did he have?

I'm not going to renege on You, he promised as night turned to day and the inhabitants of Lives began to stir. *I won't let my feelings for Cassie come between us. But please, help me.*

But for the first time in a very long time, Rick couldn't reach Heaven. An impenetrable barrier seemed to lie between him and God.

And that only added to his guilt. He was a failure.

Chapter Eight

Cassie woke, nose twitching as the aroma of coffee assailed her. Michael lay in the same position on the floor, sound asleep. His slightly improved color did nothing to curb her worry. If she had to, she could summon local help, but Cassie knew they wouldn't have the equipment needed to thoroughly evaluate and treat her patient. He needed a specialist.

She showered and dressed. On her way to the kitchen she noticed that the winter storm had almost spent itself. Hopefully it wouldn't be long before the air ambulance arrived.

"Good morning." Rick sat at the dining table, rumpled-looking, his lined face giving away his restless night. And yet, he still looked as handsome to her as he always had.

"Morning." Cassie tore her gaze away and poured a cup of coffee. When she sat down across from him, he leaned forward to peer into her face. "How are you?"

"I'm fine." She sipped her coffee, waiting for the caffeine to take effect. "Is Laurel up?"

"Yes." Rick nodded. "She's been on the phone. Apparently there was a disaster at a mine north of here and all the air ambulances have been directed there to handle the victims. Since Michael isn't in immediate danger, they've put him on a wait list."

"He can't wait," Cassie said, frustrated by the delay. "He needs to be assessed immediately, before he seizes again."

"That's what Laurel thought. That's why she's doing her best to persuade the correctional service to send a plane to take him to Winnipeg. Don't worry, Cassie." He reached across the table to cover her hand with his. A second later he pulled his hand away with a strange look on his face.

"Are you sure you're okay?" Cassie asked, confused by his actions. His expressive green eyes looked troubled.

"I'm fine." There was an edge to his voice she'd never heard before.

Why was he acting so strangely? "I guess I'd better pack a bag."

"In case you have to go with Michael?"

"I'm afraid he'll have another seizure on the way. The air ambulance would have medical staff on board, but if Laurel gets a plane and there's only a pilot…" Her voice trailed away.

Rick nodded his understanding then drew away

at the sound of voices in the hall. He probably didn't want the boys to see them huddled together. For a moment Rod teased him about not helping Teddy shovel the newly fallen snow outside, but he quickly noted Rick's serious expression. A hush fell as the boys quietly took their places at the table.

"Is M-Michael o-o-kay?" Noah asked in a sober tone.

"Yes." Cassie explained that he needed to go to Winnipeg, and that she might go with him.

"Michael gets his own plane? Man." Daniel's grin flashed. "Like a rich man."

"That's me." Michael's bitter tone resounded as he strode into the room and sat down. "The guy who gets all the breaks. Brain injuries, seizures—wow, am I lucky."

"He was just teasing, man." Rod did his best to make peace.

"I hope the plane crashes," Michael snarled. He jumped out of his chair, knocking it to the floor. The sharp crack startled everyone, including Michael. He wheeled and left the room in a rush.

"We didn't mean to bug him," Rod apologized.

"It's okay." Rick explained that Michael needed their support and prayers. He soon had the other boys agreeing to pray for Michael.

"I don't know how you do that," Cassie marveled after the boys had finished their breakfasts and left. "The way you get the boys on board with befriending Michael even though he always pushes them away—it's amazing."

"It's a matter of making them realize that they could be in Michael's shoes and need someone to rely on." He shrugged. "Everybody needs a friend."

Cassie thought about how Laurel had been her only friend for so long—until Rick. Rick seemed like the best friend she'd ever had.

Did that mean she could trust him?

"Why don't you go get ready? I'll talk to Michael," he offered.

"Thank you." Her eyes met his.

"That's what friends are for," Rick murmured.

Cassie paused in the doorway and turned to look directly at him, searching his eyes. "Is that what we are?" she asked before she could stop herself.

Rick stopped chewing. He set down the remainder of his toast, then said, "What else could we be, Cassie?"

It wasn't so much his question that bothered Cassie. It was the tone underlying his words—it sounded almost like a warning. Did he think she expected more than friendship from him? Would he reject more? Confused, she left the room.

As she was packing, she puzzled over her reaction to his question. She felt dismayed, even disappointed. Why?

Because in her heart of hearts, she thought of Rick as more than a friend.

The knowledge startled Cassie so much that she stayed in her room until she heard Laurel calling her. By then she was eager to leave, eager to escape the miasma of questions Rick had caused.

"A plane for Michael will be here within the hour," Laurel told her.

"I'm ready," she said. She sought out Rick, who was now alone in the family room.

"I want to ask you a favor. Would you please watch out for Noah?" she asked, even as she wondered if it was a mistake, if that comment earlier about being friends was his way of trying to communicate to her that he wanted distance. "I'm worried he'll get in a fight—"

"Cassie." Rick rested his hand on her shoulder. "You don't have to be afraid. God has His hand on that boy. I'll be here if Noah needs me. Trust me."

Trust me.

"Thank you," she said with heartfelt gratitude.

Part of her hated to leave. Questions about Rick plagued her. But another part of her was afraid he didn't want anything more to do with her. The very idea filled her with sadness and she realized that Rick had become a large part of her world.

Cassie felt Rick's gaze follow her as she grabbed her bag. His hand covered hers as he took it from her and they headed out to the car with Michael and Laurel. Rick helped Michael into his seat and offered his iPod with music for the boy to listen to. Before he got into the driver's seat, he leaned in to check on Cassie in the passenger's seat. His face came so near to hers, Cassie had to force herself not to reach out and cup his cheek in her palm.

Trust me.

At the last second, Cassie touched his hand and leaned forward.

"I do trust you, Rick."

His eyes blazed a brilliant jade-green. A smile stretched across his face. For a brief second, Cassie thought she saw sadness in his smile. Then he took her hand in his. "You won't be sorry you did, Cassie."

She hoped not.

"We've had two storms in the two days since you left. Somehow you've managed to return before the next one hits," Laurel informed her as she drove Cassie to Lives from the airport. "Michael comes back when?"

"A week, maybe." Cassie gazed at the beauty of the white landscape blazing in the winter sun. Funny how good it felt to leave Winnipeg. Funny how it felt as if she was coming home.

Funny how much she wanted to see Rick.

"That is, a week if he does okay on his new medication."

Cassie didn't hear much of the rest of Laurel's comments. She was too anxious to see Noah again, to make sure he was safe. To make sure Rick had kept his promise. So when they pulled into the yard she jumped out, grabbed her case and hurried inside Lives.

As she set the bag in the foyer, she heard Rick's voice in the family room. Her silly heart bounced with joy when she found him and Noah together, focused on a chessboard.

"Hi, Mom," Noah said. His smile flashed at her.

"Hi, yourself." She bent and hugged him, surprised that he not only allowed it but he returned it. Stunned, she stood back to survey him. Her son seemed calmer. Her eyes met Rick's. Whatever wariness she'd seen in him before she left was gone now. "How are you, Rick?"

"Getting beaten to a pulp by this guy," he said with a growl at Noah. "Otherwise I'm fine. Michael?"

"He's on some new medication. Once he's settled into it, he should start feeling better." Cassie sat down. "And everyone else?"

"Fine as frog's hair, as an old friend used to say." Rick kept staring at her, as if he couldn't get enough of watching her. Cassie felt the same. Finally he broke the connection between them when Noah reminded him it was his turn. He moved his piece too quickly and Noah seized it, checkmating him. "See what I mean?" he groaned.

"I keep t-telling you, y-you have to concentrate." Noah rolled his eyes. "You always f-forget."

"Yes, I do," Rick agreed, his gaze returning to Cassie.

"Do you have homework, son?" Cassie asked. When Noah nodded she raised one eyebrow. Without a single argument, Noah rose, thanked Rick for the game then left. Cassie looked at Rick. "What have you done with the real Noah?"

Rick shrugged.

"I'm serious. It sounds like he's stuttering less and he's certainly less belligerent. No problems?"

"Nary a one. We've been talking a lot. I think he's begun to heal, maybe." Rick smiled, then tilted his head to study her. "You look rested."

"I feel rested. Once I got Michael to the hospital, the staff took over. There were some long consultations with his doctors but other than that, I was free until the plane left today. I managed a little wool shopping." Cassie chuckled when he rolled his eyes. "Because the two boxes I have in my room aren't enough."

"Alicia will be glad. She's sold out of everything you made. I guess that means you'll be busy for a while." Rick's smile flashed again. "As if that's anything new."

"Anything interesting happen while I was gone?" she asked.

"Some of the kids who don't want to sing in the choir asked if they can form a band. Kyle's been encouraging it by pounding on a set of drums." Rick rolled his eyes. "Lucy's gotten on board, too, with her latest online purchase—used instruments from a school band."

"A saxophone?" she asked hopefully.

"Not yet, but soon I hope. I've now got half the town's adolescents nagging me to get the band started."

"You wanted youth participation, right?" she teased.

His smile warmed her. It felt as if the part inside

her that had frozen hard against letting anyone get too close had begun to thaw. Cassie could hardly believe it.

"I have to make some calls. I'd better get going." Rick led the way to the front door, and Cassie caught the scent of his aftershave. She found herself inhaling deeply.

"I'll be glad when Michael returns," Rick said. "We've missed him. I don't think the boys like the change. I guess most people don't. They find it threatening."

Cassie frowned. Was Rick hinting at something?

"I appreciate your help with the choir, Cassie. A lot." He slipped his fingers into his leather gloves as if delaying looking at her.

"And I appreciate yours with Noah. Did he tell you anything I should know?"

"We mostly just talked." Rick's gaze slid away.

"Well, thank you for doing that." She kept her tone even, though something inside her went on alert.

"You're welcome." Rick seemed mesmerized by the collage of Northern Lights photos hanging on the wall above her head.

"Noah admires you," Cassie murmured. "I think he'll consider whatever advice you give him."

"I should go," Rick said somewhat suddenly.

"Wait." Cassie's bag sat in one corner, reminding her. "I brought you a present." He raised his eyebrows. "Don't get excited because it's nothing big."

"You didn't need to bring me anything," he said quietly.

"I was at the airport newsstand when I suddenly remembered all those newspapers you love to read. I know how expensive it is to get the big city papers here so I thought I'd save you some money." She zipped open her bag and lifted out a thick roll, bound with two elastic bands. "These are the two most recent Toronto papers. I thought some of the stories might be of interest. I didn't read them, though, so if they're duds, chuck 'em."

"I'm sure they'll make great reading. Thank you." Rick sounded as if he was losing his voice. He accepted the roll as if it was hot, tucked it under one arm and put his hand on the doorknob.

"Rick?"

"Yes." He finally looked directly at her. His green eyes swirled with thoughts Cassie couldn't understand.

"I just wanted to say thank you again for helping me realize I can trust you. It's a relief to know that after—" She paused, inhaled and continued. "Well, after I didn't think I could trust anyone. You've been so open and honest. That's something new for me."

"Well, that's…" He looked so uncomfortable with her praise, Cassie was about to ask him what was wrong when he exhaled deeply and said, "Cassie, I need to tell you—"

The door opened and Laurel entered.

"Hi. You're leaving?" she asked Rick. When he nodded, she said, "Probably a good idea if you want to sleep at home tonight. By the looks of it, this storm will be worse than predicted. The snow's already started."

"Then I'd better go." Rick paused. His gaze rested on Cassie for a moment longer. The hunted look she saw there confused her, but before she could ask, he pulled open the door and stepped into the swirling white world.

The door closed behind him. A moment later they heard the sound of his snowmobile roaring away.

"Rick wasn't very talkative. Is anything wrong?" Laurel glanced at Cassie as she slipped out of her coat.

"I don't know." Cassie excused herself, picked up her bag and carried it up to her room, unsettled by Rick's strange behavior. She left her bag unpacked and sat down on her window seat as old uncertainties came rushing back. Maybe she'd done something to upset him.

Her mind circled back to the newfound trust she felt for Rick. For the first time in a very long time, Cassie felt right about trusting.

"Rick's not like Eric and my father," she whispered. "He's generous and good. But—"

And that was the issue. But what came next?

Tired and confused, Cassie rose and unpacked.

But she couldn't dislodge the wobbly uncertainty in her stomach that something was wrong.

Rick raced away from Lives, his mind replaying Cassie talking about how trusting him had changed things for her. The roll of newspapers burned like a hot coal where it lay inside his snowsuit. When he got home, he dropped Cassie's gift on the floor before shedding his outdoor clothes. He tried to calm the anguish her words had aroused, to no avail.

You should have told her the truth. She deserves that.

Yes, she deserved to know. But he needed privacy to tell her the whole story—how he'd renounced his old life of greed after losing money that belonged to her father and others, turned his back on wealth, dedicated himself to God and serving Him. He needed to explain those past mistakes.

Rick tried to pray about it. But the only voice he heard inside his head reminded him, *be sure your sins will find you out.*

The truth was he'd deliberately kept his secret. Because if he'd told Cassie, he knew she would refuse to let him help Noah. The boy was finally emerging from his bitterness. He couldn't interfere with that just to appease his guilt.

A knock on his door interrupted his self-condemnation.

"What are you doing out in this weather?" Rick asked Kyle, drawing his friend inside and shutting out the snow.

"You left Lives in a rush looking pretty grim. I was worried about you." Kyle's gaze fell on the roll Rick had dropped on the floor. "Are those new?"

"Yes." Kyle gave a whoop of excitement and began unrolling them. Rick headed for the kitchen. "I'll put the kettle on—hot chocolate okay?"

When Kyle didn't answer, Rick turned. Kyle's gaze was locked on a one-page ad in the newspaper. After a moment he raised his eyes to stare at Rick.

"Yes. They're rereleasing my book." Rick swallowed.

"Is that why you've been so out of sorts lately?"

"Not exactly."

"What's going on, Rick?"

Rick took a deep breath and told Kyle about the strange connection that he and Cassie shared—that it was her father who'd saved Rick from the streets. And that Rick had gone on to lose all of her father's money for him, which he felt had caused tension between Cassie and her father after Eric had died.

"Does she know about this—?" Kyle flopped down, his eyes widening as he read the ad.

"She knows that I know John, and that John saved my life. But she doesn't know what I did to him. I was going to tell her the truth." Rick held up his hand, forefinger and thumb millimeters apart. "I was this close. Then Laurel came in. It's not the kind of thing I can explain in front of others," he defended when Kyle frowned. "I need to tell Cassie the truth in private."

"You need to tell her the truth right away," Kyle corrected. "She's going to struggle with knowing that you played a bigger role in their estrangement and kept it a secret."

"I know." Rick made the chocolate in two big mugs and handed one to Kyle. He placed his on a nearby table, unable to drink it.

"The truth always outs, pal. Always."

"I know. It's just hard to think of myself as that greedy jerk, even harder to explain it to someone else. Cassie's father was the only thing between me and death so many times."

"Did you tell her that?" Kyle leaned back, his mug in his hand.

"I told her some of it, but not all. After I hit bottom, Cassie's father was the one who introduced me to the Savior." Rick shook his head. "I'd never have made it but for John. I was hoping Cassie would see that maybe she misjudged her father, that maybe she didn't know the whole story."

"And?" Kyle leaned forward.

"I'm not sure. She hasn't said anything about him for a while, and I haven't wanted to bring him up, for obvious reasons." He shook his head sadly. "The sad thing is, Kyle, John adored his daughter. He was so proud of the way she struggled to keep strong in her faith after her mom died. When I last saw him a year ago, I guessed there was some resentment between them, but I never imagined they would stop speaking."

"Money can do that to relationships. Sara told

me Cassie's dad calls every week but she mostly doesn't speak to him. That can't go on." Kyle tipped up his mug, swallowed the last of his hot chocolate, then rose. "For Noah's sake, if not for her own, Cassie needs to rebuild that relationship. She might not admit it but she needs her father. You're a minister. Your job is to help facilitate Cassie's healing."

Rick hadn't known about the phone calls, but now that he did, it only added to his guilt and fueled his determination to find a way to tell Cassie the truth.

Kyle didn't hesitate. He led out in a plea for God's leading, direction, preparation of Cassie's heart and for Rick to find the words he needed to say. Finished praying, he clapped a hand on Rick's back. "I know this will be a delicate talk. She might be furious at you. Any number of things might happen. But don't put this off, Rick. Tell her the truth. If you don't, it will only get worse." Kyle glanced at the newspaper and then at Rick. "There's something else we need to discuss. Are you falling for Cassie?"

Rick paused to consider his answer. The wind outside howled, rattling the windows with fury, causing a tinkling sound as it threw icy particles against the glass.

"I care about her," Rick admitted finally.

"Care, how? Like a pastor? Like a friend? Or more than that?" Kyle rose. "You don't need to tell me but I do think you need to figure out what you expect from her."

"I know." Rick glanced out the window. "It's gotten much worse out there," he said. "Are you sure you can make it home?"

"Are you kidding? I've been getting around Churchill since I was a kid. I could find my way blindfolded." Kyle pulled on his snowmobile helmet. "Thanks for sharing," he said, his voice muffled.

"Thanks for listening. Have Sara call when you get home. I want to know I won't have to go searching tonight." Rick waited until Kyle nodded.

"Such a worrier," he teased. Then he yanked open the door and strode into the storm.

Rick listened for the roar of the snowmobile's engine, then closed the door. After Sara called to say Kyle was home safely, Rick turned off the lights, sank onto his sofa and stared into the storm that swept across the bay.

"I care about her," he whispered, looking toward the heavens. "A lot. More than an objective pastor should. But I know what I promised You. I'm not going to act on my feelings because nothing can happen between us and I don't want to hurt her."

But Rick couldn't see a way around causing pain to the woman he cared about. In fact, after he told her that he was the reason her father had no money—either for her or for himself—it was very likely that Cassie Crockett would hate him.

Rick tried to pray for strength and the right words to confess. But as the storm outside raged, all he heard was Cassie's sweet voice, and those words that caused him to hang his head in shame.

I trust you, Rick.

Chapter Nine

"Cassie this is stunning. I've never seen such creativity with yarn."

Alicia Featherstone lifted the piece Cassie had just finished, her fingers deft but inquisitive as she examined the sweater once meant for Eric. "Did you bring anything else?"

"An afghan. I was inspired by the Northern Lights' display we had a couple of weeks ago." She waited anxiously while Alicia examined the throw. "Are they suitable?"

"Suitable? They're amazing." Alicia tilted her head to one side. "Can you do some kids' things?"

"Sure." Cassie looked into Alicia's dark eyes and wished she could unburden her heart.

"You seem troubled. Is something wrong?"

"I'm just confused and mixed up." Cassie prepared to leave, but Alicia persuaded her to stay and share a coffee at the tiny table in the rear of the store.

"Please tell me what's wrong. I'd like to help if I can." Alicia handed her a steaming cup. "Is it Rick?"

"Why do you say that?" Had everyone noticed that she couldn't seem to stay away from him?

"Just a guess. You help him a lot with the choir and now the band he's started." Alicia smiled. "Besides, he's a very nice guy. I can understand why you'd care for him."

"I think I care," Cassie admitted. "But I don't really trust him. I want to but—" After a gentle prod from Alicia, Cassie poured out her story. "Dad, Eric, God—I feel like they all betrayed me and I don't want to be tricked again," she ended.

"God will never betray you, Cassie. I don't believe Rick would, either." Alicia frowned. "I don't know anything about relationships so maybe I'm off base, but it seems to me that it isn't that you're afraid to trust Rick. It sounds more like you don't want to trust him in case you get hurt again."

"I think you're pretty smart about relationships," Cassie murmured.

"Well, my friend Sara says that if you love someone, you have to be willing to expose yourself to hurt because people are human. But she says loving and getting hurt are better than not loving at all. Do you know what I mean?"

"I think so." Cassie smiled at her. "Thank you, Alicia. It was good to talk to someone."

"Pray about it. God will give you the answer.

And don't worry that I'll tell anyone," Alicia said. "It'll be a secret between friends."

"Thank you." Cassie hugged her, finished her coffee and left. Then she visited the bank. Thanks to Alicia, her savings account was growing by leaps and bounds.

She drove back to Lives, bellowing out a praise tune she'd learned when she was a little kid, her heart somehow lighter.

She owed Rick big-time. In the past week since she'd come back from Winnipeg, she'd seen glimpses of a different Noah, thanks to the special bond that Rick and Noah seemed to have going.

Rick had brought up the subject of her father twice, but Cassie cut him off both times. This was her new life. She didn't want to be dragged back into her painful past and those feelings of being blamed. Yet, Noah was asking about his grandfather more often now, making Cassie wonder if reconciling would help her son shed whatever still plagued him. And, face it, she missed her dad. Alicia was right, loving was better than not.

When Cassie drove into the yard at Lives, her heart jumped inside her chest at the sight of Rick's snowmobile. She scolded herself for behaving like a teenager, but she knew it wouldn't change a thing.

Every time Rick was around, her emotions ran amok. She prodded her brain to remember her promise never to let anyone get that close again, but her brain ignored that. As Cassie walked to the door, her step grew a bit lighter in anticipation of seeing him.

Inside, noises from the family room intrigued her. She took off her coat and followed the sounds, helpless to stop her smile from widening when she saw Rick. Thankfully he didn't notice because he was busy trying to show Daniel some dance steps. And failing miserably. She couldn't help chuckling out loud.

"Ah." Rick's eyes gleamed. He held out a hand. "Just the person we need to get you fellows up to speed for the Valentine's Day dance. Now you guys watch and Cassie and I will show you how it's done."

Dance with him? Her mouth went completely dry. But Rick gave her no time to refuse.

"Start that music over, Rod," he ordered. He grabbed her hand, drew her close and grinned. "Ready?"

Cassie nodded, falling into the movement and rhythm of the music with an ease that surprised her. She'd loved to dance from the moment her mother had taken her to her very first ballet class. Dancing was something she'd shared with Eric when they were first married, until he became too busy to keep their weekly date night. It had been years, but as Cassie followed Rick's lead around the room, the joy of moving to music surged back. Worries and burdens melted away as she reveled in his strong yet gentle arm at her back.

"This is how it's done, guys," Rick said. His green eyes met hers. "You dance beautifully," he murmured.

For days now Cassie had felt some hesitation in Rick, something she couldn't quite put her finger on. But now she sensed that Rick was into this perfect moment as much as she was. The music carried her into a daydream world where she and Rick shared and laughed and enjoyed, a world that stretched into a future of possibility. She wanted it to go on and on, but the music ended too soon.

Cassie looked up and got trapped in Rick's searching gaze. It bored deep inside her, asking questions to which she had no answers, telling her something she couldn't quite grasp.

She was loath to move away until a burst of applause broke the spell. Then Rick released her. A draft of chilly air took the place of his warm embrace. He stepped back, bowed to her and then turned to the boys.

"So that's your goal," he told them, his voice slightly raspy. He looked her way, but the emotions she'd glimpsed in his eyes mere seconds ago were now hidden. "Would you mind helping the boys, Cassie? They seem to believe a few pre-lessons at home will make them look less awkward on the dance floor."

Cassie nodded, unable to speak. How Rick could seem so unaffected by their dance was a mystery. Cassie was thankful that he partnered her first with Noah. She needed some time to get her senses under control. Noah caught on to the steps quickly, despite his cast. Perhaps the impromptu dances she'd drawn him into when he was younger—times when Cassie desperately needed to feel alive and vital and carefree—had paid off. After a few minutes, Noah stepped away from her.

"I g-got it now, M-Mom. You'd b-better help, R-Rod. He l-looks like a g-geek."

"Hey!" Rod glared at him, his face dark red.

Cassie obliged, trying not to wince after Rod stepped on her toes for the hundredth time. When she glanced at Noah, she saw him peering out the window, his face gloomy and shadowed with his thoughts. She was going to ask Rod if he knew why when Rick broke them up to pair her with Daniel, who was also not happy.

"This is slow and pokey," he muttered, his hand fisted against her waist. "Nobody dances like this but old people."

"Don't you want to learn to dance, Daniel?" But Cassie knew it wasn't that. She could see in his eyes that he was battling a craving for drugs. He needed something to work it off. "Rick," she called. "Can you put on something faster?"

Rick's gaze met hers. He nodded, and a moment later an energetic tune filled the room.

"Okay now, Daniel. Concentrate." Cassie grabbed his hand and swung him into a two-step. Daniel floundered for a moment or two but he was a quick study and before the end of the song he was fully into it, moving easily, his face aglow.

"You, my boy, are a natural dancer," Cassie puffed as she caught her breath while the other boys clapped for them. "You've got a sense of rhythm that a lot of people don't possess. You should do something with it."

"Really?" Daniel looked startled.

"Cassie's right, kid. You've got the moves," Rick told him with a grin. "Now, how about you give someone else a chance?"

Daniel nodded and sat down with a proud smile as he watched the other boys clumsily learn the basic steps. Michael, whom she'd welcomed back this morning, was the last one. He shuffled toward Cassie, looking listless.

"Are you feeling okay, Michael?" she asked as she took his hand.

"Fine," he said, moving slowly to the jazz tune Rick had chosen. "But I'd rather be playing the sax to this than dancing."

"I know. Rick and I haven't given up on that. We'll find you one, I promise."

At one point Cassie glanced at Rick and found him staring at Michael, his forehead creased, his eyes narrowed. She was fairly certain his thoughts matched hers.

"I'm sorry I got called away." Laurel's voice drew their attention to the doorway as the music ended. "From what I just saw, I think we owe Rick and Cassie a big thank-you," she said and led the others in a burst of applause. "I don't think any of you will embarrass Lives Under Construction at the Valentine's Day dance," she teased. She then invited everyone to come for supper.

Cassie hung back with Rick and Laurel as the boys rushed to the table. "I'm worried about Michael."

"So am I," Laurel murmured. "But I don't know what else we can do."

"I might." Rick smiled at their surprise. "Leave it to me, okay? I've got an idea I want to try."

"Your ideas are a blessing to us." Laurel wrapped her arms around him in a brief hug. "I don't know what we'd do without you."

"Hopefully you won't have to find out," he joked. He turned to Cassie. "Will you be able to make choir practice tomorrow?"

"My schedule's clear so far." Cassie thought she'd heard a trace of desperation in his voice. "I'll be there after school."

"Excellent. I'd better go. I've got Bible study tonight."

"You won't stay for supper?" Laurel asked.

"I'll have to take a rain check," he said. "Thanks, though."

"You're always welcome," Laurel assured him. After a sideways glance at Cassie, she walked toward the kitchen.

"I need to thank you, too," Cassie said. "I deposited a lovely check today and that's thanks to you for suggesting I see Alicia. I'm gradually building back my savings."

"Good." But Rick's green eyes looked troubled as they rested on her.

"Is anything wrong?" she asked.

"Cassie, I—"

She waited, breathless, for what she didn't know. He shook his head. "Never mind. This isn't the time."

Frustrated, Cassie followed him to the door. "I'll see you tomorrow at practice then," she said.

"You will." He smiled absentmindedly then left.

Cassie stood in the doorway, watching him drive away until the cold air forced her to shut the door.

Something's going on with him, something he doesn't want to tell me about.

Later that evening, Cassie sat in the window seat in her room, knitting. The moon, round and full, illuminated the glistening snow. She could see for miles across the tufted tundra as she relived what it felt like to be in Rick's arms. She remembered the tender way he'd whispered in her ear, felt the sweet pressure of his hand against her back when they'd danced. Oh, how she'd wanted it to continue.

I love him. How had it happened? How had Rick Salinger made it past the barriers she'd erected after Eric's death?

Cassie had no answers. All she knew was that Rick had pushed the pain and sadness out of her heart. She felt alive, ready to take on her future. Maybe it *was* time to talk to her father, to try to rebuild their bond. Not just for Noah, but for herself, too.

Cassie took out a piece of stationery and her favorite pen. Worry gripped her. What if her father didn't want to reconcile? What if he only wanted to talk to Noah?

When I was a child I talked like a child, I thought like a child, I reasoned like a child; now that I have grown up, I am done with childish ways and have put them aside.

The old familiar passage from First Corinthians pushed out the doubts. Wasn't it time she grew up? Wasn't it time to have some faith in God's love? For the first time in ages, Cassie bowed her head.

"Please help me," she whispered. "I need my dad. I need my family. I need You."

I need Rick.

Cassie wanted to beg God to take away the sprout of love that had taken root inside her heart. She wanted to, but she couldn't. Rick had become too big a part of her world, too important to her happiness.

She'd told him she trusted him.

It was time to trust God, too.

Dear Dad. She paused, then began to write, pouring out her heart on paper.

Chapter Ten

"Boy I'm glad to see you." Rick heaved a sigh of relief the next afternoon when Cassie rushed through the church door for the first rehearsal with the band and the choir together. Seeing her lovely face made him so happy, he felt like a giddy teenager.

"I'm sorry I'm late." She sounded breathless as she unwound her scarf and pulled off her jacket and gloves. "Would you believe Laurel's van wouldn't start?"

"Yes, I would." He grinned. "That vehicle needs to be replaced." He waited until she was seated at the piano. "Do you want to run over it before we begin?"

"I think I'll be okay," Cassie said. "I'm ready whenever you are."

"Good." Rick tapped his music stand to gain the kids' attention, waiting until all eyes were on him.

"Ready? Here we go. Wait for Cassie's introduction." He nodded to her to begin. "Now."

Most of the choir managed to hit the first note but the band members straggled in late so he started again. It was only marginally better the second time but Rick pressed on, leading them to the end without stopping. As the last note died away, the kids remained silent for a moment. Then everyone rushed to speak.

"We did it!" they exclaimed in proud surprise.

"Of course you did." Rick shared a grin with Cassie. "We have to remember those pauses where the choir sings without the band. But if we practice, I know we can have it perfect in time for Easter morning. Doesn't it make a difference having Cassie play for us?"

The kids concurred, eager to try again. After they finished the third run-through, they drooped, exhilarated but obviously tired. Rick praised their efforts effusively, reminded them of the next practice and then dismissed them. Cassie rose as if she, too, would leave.

This was the moment.

"Can I talk to you for a few minutes?" he asked. "Privately?"

Cassie's eyebrows rose in surprise but she nodded and began to put away her music. Once the last boy had wandered out, she looked at him, a question in her eyes.

"You've done an amazing job," Rick said. Her eyes still shone with the passion she'd poured into her playing. "I think this Easter is going to be very special."

"Me, too. I can't believe how much you've done with them," Cassie said. Rick's pride surged at her praise. "Noah sounds amazing. You were right— his stutter completely disappears when he sings."

"He's remarkable." Rick sat down in the front pew facing her. "They all are. I wish I could do more."

"More? Like what?" Her pretty smile flashed. "Get them doing a full-scale opera?"

"I doubt they'd agree to that," he said, laughing a little. "No, I meant I need to find something for Michael other than those bells. I need to find a saxophone and so far I'm hitting a wall."

Quit prevaricating. He exhaled. He opened his mouth.

"I wrote my dad, Rick." Cassie said it softly, quietly, studying him as she spoke. "I did what you said and told him how I felt abandoned by him."

"How do you feel about that?" he asked, relieved to put off his confession a little longer.

"Good. Calmer. As if a big block in my life has dissolved." Her surprise was obvious. "I guess I never realized just how much my anger about him was bothering me."

"It is surprising when we let go of something and then realize the hold it had on us," he agreed. "God answers prayer, Cassie. And He knows how to work this out."

"I haven't had much success with talking to God lately," she admitted, her eyes avoiding his.

"That's not unusual. When you haven't talked in a while, it takes some time to regain the closeness you used to share." He saw that mystified look on her face. "You have to purposefully rebuild your relationship with God, just like you do with your dad. Eventually you'll get to a point where you'll be able to declare something."

"Like what?"

"Like declaring that you'll trust God." He said it deliberately, knowing how shaky her trust was but wanting her to take another step. Cassie frowned.

"Even if I'm not sure I can?" she murmured. "I keep going back, Rick. I keep thinking maybe, if I'd been a better wife, paid more attention, if I'd seen Eric's desperation to impress his board, maybe I could have prevented his suicide."

"Looking back is useless. There's nothing you can do to change what happened, Cassie." He paused, waiting for some heavenly direction. But it wasn't there. Was it because his attraction to Cassie meant he was betraying his promise to God? "God knew what would happen," he said, struggling to find the words. "And He gave you the strength to get through it."

"I don't understand." She shook her head. "If He knew how much it would hurt, why did He let it happen?" A tear spilled down her cheek. "Why did I have to go through all that pain?"

Rick hesitated. He was a pastor. He was supposed to be able to help her, lead her so she could find God's love again. Yet he felt weighed down by his own guilt.

"I don't know why it had to happen that way, Cassie. But *why* doesn't really matter now, does it?" His own words sounded hollow as he moved from the pew to hunker down in front of her. He took her hand in his. "I see your struggle as a test. You've come this far. Now you need to decide if you're going to lose your faith or if you're going to fight for it."

"How do I do that?" Her eyes implored him for help.

This is why God placed me in Churchill.

Rick blocked out every emotion. He was determined to help Cassie through this.

"Whenever you talk about the past, your body language changes," he began. "Your shoulders hunch, you tighten up and your smile disappears. Your words are tight, tense and short."

"I know. That's how I feel," Cassie admitted.

"But if you could see yourself when you're with your patients," he continued. "Your face is relaxed, your voice is soft. You're open and trusting." Rick smiled as images of her just like that filled his mind.

"How is that connected to my faith?" She frowned.

"I think you need to treat yourself like you treat your patients," he said. "You need new words to reframe the way you talk about the past and help you look to the future." Cassie's eyebrows rose high, as if that was the last thing she expected from him. "You need to be gentle with yourself. Because that's the way God feels toward you."

"Go on." She was still frowning, but he could see that he had her attention.

"Words are powerful and whether we realize it or not, what we say impacts the way we live our lives. I'm suggesting you start reframing your life and your faith with the way you speak."

Cassie slowly withdrew her hand from his. Rick rose, stepped back and sat beside her on the front pew.

"That sounds reasonable."

"It is. But if you're going to do that, you need to start with a basic premise," he added. "How about God is love?"

Cassie took a long time to think about it before she nodded.

"So because God is love and wants only the best for us, we trust Him." Rick forced his mind off the way her curls tumbled onto her face like shavings of gold, illuminating her lovely skin. "He teaches us to do that by giving us tests that will help stretch our faith. We might not like it, but we know that God has something good in mind. He's answering our prayer and we just haven't realized it yet."

"You're talking about the power of positive thinking," she said.

"Oh, no." Rick shook his head. "I'm talking about speaking the truths God gave us in His word and being confident in Him instead of letting the storms we go through control our emotions and thoughts."

"I'm not sure I follow."

"The best way to keep our trust in God is to remember His promises. 'I can do all things through Christ who strengthens me.'" Rick paused—he needed a moment to absorb the beauty of Cassie beginning to claim her faith. "'All things work together for good to those who love God and are called according to His purpose,'" he quoted.

"'I am more than a conqueror through Christ who strengthens me,'" Cassie quoted in return. The gold in her eyes began to glow. "'I will not fear, for God is with me.'"

Rick could only nod as realization of her position with God dawned on Cassie. He'd always thought she was beautiful, but now she was stunning as she radiated God's love. She repeated verse after verse, her voice filling the sanctuary, growing stronger as her faith grew.

When she stopped speaking, her eyes met his. Rick couldn't move. There could be nothing between them—he knew that and mourned it—but that didn't stop his heart from surging with joy at her renewal as a child of God.

"I'm beginning to understand," Cassie whispered as a smile spread across her face. "I get it."

This woman was a jewel beyond compare. Rick could no more ignore the affection he felt for her than he could have ignored her pleas for help.

Until he realized his own test was going to be giving her up.

"Just keep your thoughts and mind centered on God and His love for you," he said, knowing he couldn't put off telling her any longer.

"Sounds easier than it is," she said shyly.

"Yes, but you can do it." He inhaled deeply. "I wanted to talk to you about something else," he said.

The back door of the church slammed. They both turned to see Noah standing there.

"Are you f-finished, Mom?" he asked. "I've g-got a lot of h-homework."

"Sorry, Rick. Another time?" Cassie asked.

He held her coat while she slipped into it. For the merest fraction of a second he allowed his hands to linger on her arms, wishing he had the right to draw her close, knowing she'd never want that after he told her the truth.

"Can I take you out for coffee tomorrow?" he asked, hearing the desperation in his voice.

"I'm on nights tonight and tomorrow so I'll be sleeping during the day," she explained, searching his gaze. "Friday is the dance. I said I'd help the boys get ready in the afternoon, and I'm chaperoning at the dance that night. Maybe we can figure out another time."

"I hope so." The need to straighten things out so that nothing but the total truth lay between them nagged at Rick. But he would have to wait. For a little while longer he could enjoy their friendship.

Friendship?

"I loved playing today." Cassie leaned forward to touch his arm. "I know I told you I didn't want to go inside a church again, but I'm very glad I did. Will you pray for me?" she asked, keeping her voice too low for Noah to hear.

"Of course." Rick yearned to reach out and brush his fingers against her cheek, to hug her close, just for a moment. Instead, aware of Noah watching, he contented himself with a platitude. "Keep trusting, Cassie. Have faith in God's love."

"That is at the root of everything, isn't it?" She studied him, then gave him a smile. "Gotta go. Bye."

"See you." Rick watched Cassie leave the church with a myriad of emotions swirling inside, the strongest of which was a soul-deep yearning to be with her.

If only—

Rick stared at the cross hanging at the front of the church. God had sacrificed so much for him. How could he ask God to forget his vow to never get romantically involved? How could he forget the debt he owed?

He couldn't. But oh, how he wanted to. Certain now that Cassie and Noah could never be the family he'd longed for all these years, Rick knelt and prayed for strength to make the confession he needed to make.

But he also asked God to be with Cassie, to smooth the way so she wouldn't see him as the scoundrel he was when he told her he had lost all her father's money.

And made it nearly impossible for John to be there for his daughter in her moment of greatest need.

"How come you're not getting ready for the Valentine's dance, Noah?"

Cassie stood in the doorway of the computer room. She frowned when her son quickly shut down whatever he was looking at.

"What were you looking at?"

"Just eBay. I wanted to ch-check something out." He stood up and tried to get past her to leave the room.

"You want to buy something?" Sensing this was important, Cassie held her ground, refusing to move out of the doorway. "What?"

"N-nothing." he said. When she still didn't budge, he shrugged. "R-Rick's guitar."

"Rick's guitar is on eBay? For sale?" Noah nodded. "But he loves that guitar. A friend in seminary gave it to him. Why would he sell it?"

Noah lowered his voice. "I think R-Rick is t-trying to get a s-saxophone for M-Michael."

"By selling his guitar?" Her heart swelled with different emotions—pride that Rick was concerned enough to give up his beloved possession, tenderness over the fact that he wouldn't ask for help but instead found a way on his own, and sadness that she and the boys would no longer be able to watch him play as he led the group in praise.

Rick, the perpetual giver, had spent much time with Michael since he'd returned to Lives, trying to help him break through his depression. He'd said he had an idea of a way to help. But to give up his most precious possession...

"He's selling it because he doesn't have enough money to buy a saxophone, you mean."

Noah nodded.

A sense of loss filled her. She shook her head. "That is a very generous thing for Rick to do."

"I know." Noah nodded. "C-can we buy it, M-Mom?"

"Buy it?" As Cassie studied Noah's earnest face, understanding flowed. "And give it back, you mean? That's such a lovely idea, Noah, but we can't afford it, honey. It would empty our savings."

"S-so? We can s-save again," he said. "I d-don't need anything."

"It's very kind of you to say that and I'm so proud of you for thinking of it." She reached for him, and suppressed the sting of rejection when he rejected her embrace. "But I have to be responsible, honey. If I bought that guitar, it would leave us with no money. What if something happened?"

Noah's disappointment was written all over his face.

"I'm so sorry, Noah," she said, laying a hand on his shoulder. "I want to help Rick as much as you do, but I simply can't do this."

"Y-yeah. I f-figured." He shrugged off her hand. "D-don't tell a-anyone. R-Rick doesn't kn-know I know." Then he bolted from the room.

Alone, Cassie thought of Rick strumming his guitar, lost in another world, a place where he found solace and peace…

Be bold and strong. Banish fear and doubt! For remember, the Lord your God is with you wherever you go.

The words she'd read from Joshua just this morning convicted Cassie. Rick asked so little for himself, yet he gave so much. Who gave to him?

"Okay, God," she murmured. "This is trust in action."

Cassie sat down in front of a computer and searched eBay until she found what she wanted. Then, holding her breath, she made a bid.

I hope you haven't made a mistake, whispered the voice inside her head.

Cassie shut it down. In her innermost heart, she knew buying back Rick's guitar wasn't a mistake. She could always knit another sweater, work another shift. She was good at finding ways to build up a nest egg.

But it wasn't every day that an opportunity came along to do something wonderful for Rick.

And Rick definitely deserved wonderful.

Rick stood in the shadows of the school auditorium, unashamedly listening to Cassie's conversation with Lucy as they manned the punch bowl at the Valentine's dance.

"So you're playing for the Easter cantata with the choir," Lucy said. "Does that mean you'll be coming to church regularly?"

"I'm not sure," Cassie said with some hesitation. "I'm not really much of a churchgoer. I believe in God but I prefer to meet with Him on my own."

Rick winced, knowing Lucy was not going to like this answer.

"What good does that do?" Lucy demanded.

"I don't know what you mean." Cassie sounded confused.

"The Bible tells us not to forsake the assembling of ourselves—in other words, church!" Lucy was ramping up. Rick had to intervene and rescue Cassie.

He stepped forward and grinned at them. "What kind of punch do we have here?"

"Red," Lucy told him unhelpfully. She handed him a glass. "I was telling Cassie that it's part of a Christian's duty to be faithful at church."

"Lucy, everyone has to come to church in their own way, in their own time," Rick said gently, trying to defuse Lucy's hard-nosed approach.

"Well, when will that be?" Lucy asked Cassie.

"I, um, don't think I'm ready yet." Cassie glanced at Lucy, her face thoughtful. "Some church members accused me of being involved in my husband's wrongdoing. I thought they should have known the truth because they knew me so I didn't dispute their claims. Now I'm wondering if maybe I should have."

"Why?" Lucy asked.

"Because I realize now that doing so might have made things easier for Noah," Cassie admitted. "If I'd publicly disputed their claims instead of avoiding confrontation, he might not have kept everything pent up inside. Maybe he wouldn't stutter now. I don't know."

"That's the thing. You never know. You do your best and you leave it in the Lord's hands. But you can share it with your Christian friends. We'll understand." Lucy clasped Cassie's hands between her own. "That's why we all admire Rick so much. He helps make our burdens lighter."

Rick felt his cheeks heat.

"I've often wished I had Rick's faith," Cassie admitted to Lucy.

"Rick gained his faith by learning from his mistakes," Lucy said.

"Hey. I'm right here, you know."

They ignored him.

"That's the way we all learn," Lucy told her.

"I don't think Rick's made as many mistakes as I have," Cassie murmured.

If she only knew, he thought.

"Come on," he said, grabbing her hand. "Let's dance. Okay?" he asked Lucy.

She grinned her know-it-all grin and nodded.

"The doubts are back, huh?" Rick asked as he threaded his arm around Cassie's waist. Cassie fit in his arms so perfectly. Their steps across the floor matched as if they'd rehearsed.

"I'm afraid my failure to defend myself was what damaged Noah," she whispered. "I wonder if it did so much damage he'll never get over his speech impediment."

"Your dad once lent me a book about a man named Sidney Cox. He wrote a song you probably know," Rick said, ignoring the guilt that rose up in him at the mention of her father. He paused a moment, then said the words in a very soft voice, "'My Lord knows the way through the wilderness. All I have to do is follow. Strength for today is mine all the way and all that I need for tomorrow.'"

"I remember that." Cassie sighed. He tried to ignore the feel of her head resting on his shoulder. "You're telling me to keep the faith, is that it?"

"Basically, yes." He felt her shoulders shake and knew she was laughing. "What?"

"Do you ever stop being a pastor?" Cassie asked.

Rick couldn't answer. Because if he had, he would have told her that the moment she'd begun to move with him to the music, he'd forgotten his vow, his determination to keep her at arm's length. He'd have said that with her he was simply a normal guy, thrilled to have the most beautiful woman in the world in his arms.

And then he would have told her why nothing could ever come of that.

Because she deserved the truth.

Rick opened his mouth but the words wouldn't

come. When the music ended, Cassie thanked him for the dance and went back to her work at the punch table.

His arms felt painfully empty.

Suddenly aware that he was alone on the dance floor, Rick sought out Noah, who was standing on the sidelines, watching.

"How's it going?"

Noah stared at Rick for a long moment. The silence stretched between them until another song began to play, a loud, noisy one that had the kids laughing and twisting to the beat. Then Noah grabbed Rick's arm and leaned near.

"Will y-you teach me t-to box?" he asked. "P-please?"

"Let's go talk about it." With one last glance at Cassie—looking more beautiful than his heart could stand in her black velvet suit with her golden hair framing her lovely face—Rick led the way out of the auditorium.

Chapter Eleven

Two weeks later Cassie played with her coffee cup, on tenterhooks as she waited for Rick's arrival at the restaurant. He'd called her several times to arrange a coffee date, but she kept getting called into work.

Fussing isn't going to get him here any faster, she told herself. *Calm down.*

Saying that didn't help, either. She felt anything but calm when her thoughts centered on Rick Salinger. Her feelings for this man had grown and changed. Every time she talked to him she grew increasingly certain that this man was *different,* that she could trust him as she trusted no other.

Cassie caught her breath when he strode through the door. When he called a greeting to the owner and then grinned at her, a part of her heart melted. He sat down across the table from her, his green eyes expectant. Cassie struggled to control her response to him while they waited for the server to bring his coffee.

How should she begin?

"Cat got your tongue?" Rick teased.

"I'm allergic to cats," she said, then rolled her eyes at the inane remark.

"So?" He leaned back, crossed his booted feet and waited. "You called me," he said.

"I—" She regrouped. "You said you wanted to talk to me and I need to talk to you. About something." She rolled her eyes at herself.

"About Noah?" His eyes darkened with concern on behalf of her son, but Cassie didn't stop to analyze that. She couldn't. She needed to get this said.

"About your guitar." Sorrow flashed briefly across his face before he concealed it.

"I—uh, I don't have it anymore." He blinked. "Actually I sold it."

"I know. I bought it, Rick." Cassie waited for her words to penetrate. "I'm your online buyer."

"You? But…" Dismay filled his face. "You need the money for your savings. You told me how important that is to you."

"Saving pennies isn't as important to me as you having that guitar, which you love. That instrument is part of you. The way you use it to bring joy and peace to so many—" She shook her head. "I couldn't let you sell it."

His jaw hardened as he looked away from her. "I won't take your money, Cassie."

"The deal is done." Cassie reached out to cover

his hand with hers and thought how strange it was to comfort him for once. "You have to take the money, Rick. You need it to get Michael his saxophone."

"You know?" His green eyes widened. "How—"

"Shame on you for not consulting me. This is our project. So I did my part." Cassie couldn't stifle the rest any longer. "You've already sent the guitar to Toronto, to a Mrs. Nancy Carr, right? She's my dad's next-door neighbor. Dad will bring your guitar when he comes for a visit sometime in the next few weeks."

"You've reconciled with him." He made a movement forward, as if he was going to hug her, but then he checked himself, substituting a smile instead. "Cassie, that's fantastic!"

"It is, isn't it?" she agreed, trying to ignore the silly feelings of loss that rushed over her at the missed opportunity to be in Rick's arms again, even if for a brief moment. "I got his letter yesterday. You were right, Rick," she admitted shyly. "I did misunderstand what my dad was trying to say. He was warning me not to get caught in the blame game and become bitter."

Rick squeezed her hand, then slowly let it go. "I'm so happy for you, Cassie."

"Thanks. It's not all sweetness and light, but we're both committed to working through the tough parts. There are still things I don't understand, but I realize now, thanks to you, that there's a lot about my dad that I don't know."

Rick leaned back, away from her. Something strange passed across his face, something she didn't quite catch.

"Are you pleased about your guitar, Rick?" she asked, suddenly feeling strangely shy.

"You shouldn't have done it, Cassie." His soft, low voice brimmed with respect and admiration. "I love that guitar, but I could have managed without it."

"I don't believe you should have to," she said, surprised by how strongly she felt. "That guitar is part of who you are, part of your ministry. And don't worry, Rick. Consider the money partial payment on the tithes I owe God for the past few years. Alicia will help me replenish my account in no time."

He looked dubious.

"I want Michael to have his saxophone as much as you do," she reassured him. "That's what's important. Now you can buy one, can't you?"

"I already did." She laughed as Rick grinned at her. "I'm praying it will help."

"It will, Rick. Of course it will."

"Thank you, Cassie." His words were filled with such tenderness that Cassie couldn't catch her breath for a moment. "We should go—it's nearly time for choir practice."

"Wait—weren't you the one who kept trying to make a coffee date with me? Well, here we are." She was confused by his sudden rush to leave.

"Wouldn't now be a good time? We have a few minutes to spare."

That look crossed Rick's face again as he swallowed the last of his coffee. "Let's do it another time."

Bewildered, Cassie gathered up her things. As they walked along the street toward the church, she was aware of speculative stares directed their way. The fact that people might pair them as Alicia had didn't bother her. In fact, she felt proud to be walking beside such an admirable man.

But she wondered if those curious eyes and whispered comments bothered Rick. Was that why he was maintaining a certain distance from her as they walked, careful not to brush shoulders or tease her the way he usually did?

Was he worried about his reputation, being seen with a woman who'd been married to a man who lost church funds? No matter how long the list of Rick's attributes, her past was a black mark that would work against him.

The doubts about Rick's behavior rose in Cassie's mind and would not be silenced.

Rehearsal did not go as well as previous ones had. Even Noah's normally clear, pure voice faltered in the midst of his solo. He actually missed several notes he'd never struggled with before.

Cassie wasn't sure if the problems stemmed from the fact that Rick didn't seem as focused, or because the kids were getting excited about the prospect of performing in public at the Easter morning service, which was now posted all over town. Whatever the reason, they looked as disheartened as she felt by the end of their practice session.

"Don't sweat it, guys. Everyone has a bad rehearsal now and then," Rick consoled them. "We'll do better next time."

"But Easter is only a month away," Rod said, disgruntled. "If we sound like this then everyone's going to laugh at us."

"No one's going to laugh," Rick said firmly. "We're going to be perfect for every note."

"Let's try it again," Michael said.

Rick shook his head. "We've done enough for today. We'll pick it up again next week. Stop worrying. It will come together." He smiled at them. "Go home now. It's almost time for supper."

As the kids left the sanctuary, Cassie studied Rick. He folded the pages of music he'd spread out, pausing every so often to call out a farewell. Though he'd pretended nonchalance, his eyes were dark with concern. Lines grooved deeper around his eyes. He glanced at her once, then quickly looked away, keeping his gaze averted as the kids left.

Only when Noah approached him and said something did Cassie see the faint vestige of a smile. Rick seemed to be shutting her out again, and she found herself wondering exactly what it was he wanted to talk to her about.

As she gathered her things and prepared to leave, her phone rang.

"Cassie, Laurel's trying to get hold of you," Sara said. "She rushed Daniel to the hospital. She's hoping you can meet her there."

"I'll be there in ten minutes." Cassie felt a shiver of dread walk up her spine. What now?

"Y-you'll be where?" Noah asked from behind her.

"The hospital. There's been an emergency with Daniel." She wouldn't say more until she knew more. She called to Rick. "I'm sorry to impose on you, Rick, but I wonder if you could take Noah home. Daniel's at the hospital."

"Sure, no problem. We'll go on my snowmobile. I had it tuned up this morning."

"Helmets?" she asked.

"I'm n-not a b-baby," Noah protested, his face red with anger.

"I insist everyone who rides my snowmobile wears a helmet," Rick said. "We'll be fine. We'll have supper together before I take him back."

"Thank you." Cassie turned to Noah. "Help with the dishes," she murmured sotto voce. "And remember, you need to get that geography assignment done tonight. No computer time until it's finished."

"I kn-know the r-rules," Noah snarled.

"I have to go." Cassie leaned forward to brush a kiss against Noah's cheek. It hurt so much when he reared back, avoiding her touch. She gulped down her tears and said, "I don't know when I'll get home. I love you."

Noah didn't respond.

Cassie turned to Rick. "Thank you for your help," she said quietly. Then she headed for the foyer.

"That wasn't very nice, Noah," she heard Rick say. "Your mother loves you."

"D-does she?" Noah didn't sound convinced.

There wasn't anything Cassie could do about it now, but when she got back to Lives, she would have a long, stern talk with her son and make sure he knew exactly how deeply she cared about him. And one way or another, she was going to have that private conversation with Rick, too.

Something was going on with him. It was time she figured out what it was.

"You want to go a few rounds?" Rick asked, nodding toward his spare room after they'd eaten a mostly silent meal and cleaned up. He'd hung the punching bag there, turning the place into a kind of mini gym, and he sensed that Noah could use some time with the bag to help with whatever was boiling inside him.

Noah's blue eyes sparkled as Rick helped him put on his boxing gloves. It was the first positive sign the boy had given all evening.

Noah worked out on the bag first, then they sparred. It was at least half an hour before Noah spoke.

"D-do you ever g-get so m-mad you want t-to

h-hit everybody?" Noah grunted, his face red with exertion.

"Is that how you feel?" Rick felt practically victorious when Noah nodded, finally engaging in conversation with him. "Why?"

"N-nothing's going r-right." He smashed his fist against Rick's glove. "I h-hate it h-here."

"Because?" Rick parried and feinted, moving fast to keep up with the boy's explosion of energy.

"P-people think I'm w-weird."

"What people?" Rick could sense Noah's fury like a red-hot fever. "Kids at school?" Noah nodded. "Your teachers?" Another nod. "Your mom?"

Noah gnawed on his lip. "I'd l-like to s-smash th-them all," he snarled.

The sheer animosity in those words stunned Rick so much he was unprepared for Noah's fist and it connected with his nose. Blood spurted out and pain exploded across his face.

Rick grabbed a towel and pressed it to his nose awkwardly with his gloved hand. It took a long time to stem the flow. Eventually it slowed down enough for him to toss away the towel and use his teeth to untie his gloves. Only then did it dawn on him that Noah hadn't said anything.

Rick looked at the boy. Noah had paled to an unhealthy shade of white. He began to shake, his whole body twitching.

"It's just a nosebleed, Noah. I'm fine. I should have ducked, just like I've been teaching you." Rick summoned a grin, though moving even those few muscles hurt like crazy. But Noah didn't respond.

Ripping off his gloves, Rick grasped Noah's arm and peered into his eyes. "I'm fine. No big deal."

"I'm s-sorry," Noah gulped as tears coursed down his cheeks. "I'm s-so s-sorry."

"I know." Rick unlaced the boy's gloves and removed them. He slid off the protective headgear he'd insisted on, wondering wryly why he hadn't thought of it for himself. Then he wrapped an arm around Noah's shoulder. "Let's go get a drink."

"D-don't you h-have to g-go to the h-hospital?"

"For a nosebleed? You want them to laugh at me?" He held Noah's gaze, refusing to look away as the boy searched his gaze. "I'm not made of sugar, you know."

"I d-didn't m-mean—"

"Noah." Rick stopped him. "People get hurt in boxing sometimes. I warned you about that before we ever started, remember?" He waited for Noah's nod. "Anyway, I'm fine. Almost."

Noah flopped down on a chair in front of the windows. Rick sat down across from him.

"Want to tell me what makes you so angry you're beating up kids at school?"

Noah's head jerked up. "You know?"

"I've suspected for a while. Something's clearly eating at you, Noah. Let's get it out in the open." He prayed silently for God to give him the right words. "Talk to me. I only want to help."

"I'm not going to be hurt anymore," Noah said

in a tight voice. "I'm not going to be made fun of ever again. If someone tries, I'll stop it."

Aghast at the admissions he was hearing, Rick sat silent, knowing Noah needed the release this honesty would bring. But the more he heard, the more he wondered— Why? What lay beneath the boy's pain?

The phone rang.

"Rick, is Noah still there?" Cassie's voice, breathless and worried came across the line.

"Yes." Just hearing her voice sent his every sense into high alert. *Get in control.* "I was about to take him to Lives," Rick told her.

"No! Don't do that." She inhaled. "I need a very big favor. Can Noah stay with you overnight, Rick?"

"Sure. What's the problem?"

"Meningitis." That one word drove all other thoughts out of his head. "Daniel has symptoms of bacterial meningitis. If that's what it is, it's very contagious. I don't want Noah to return to Lives and risk any more exposure than he already has. He's okay, isn't he?"

"He's fine." Rick caught Noah watching him. The kid rolled his eyes and shook his head, as if annoyed by his mother's concern. "You take care of yourself and your patients. I'll watch out for Noah."

"Thank you." Silence stretched between them for a moment, and then her voice dropped. "Rick?"

"I'm here."

"Can you pray? Hard. All the kids were probably exposed, but if Michael catches it…" Her voice trailed away and in that moment the severity of the situation hit him full force.

Meningitis was serious. Noah and Michael had both been exposed.

But so had Cassie.

Rick felt as if the world stopped. She was around sick people all the time. Hospital viruses were often the most dangerous. She could catch this thing herself and—die?

God, no.

"I know it's a lot to ask you," she whispered in a broken tone. "You probably had plans for tonight and I'm ruining them and—"

"Cassie," he said softly. "Noah and I will be praying. You can count on that. And on God," he added, hoping to bolster her fledgling faith. "God knows what's at stake. He's right there with you."

He scolded himself for falling back on a standby platitude and thought what a sham he'd become. He was supposed to be ministering to her, yet his own doubts were derailing him.

"Thank you, Rick. I mean that."

Rick held the phone long after she'd hung up. Tenderness rushed over him in a wave of appreciation for this precious woman who took to heart the welfare of the boys at Lives and her patients while she worried for her own son.

How can I shut her out, God? How am I supposed to ignore her when my heart wants to be with her always, when every day that I don't talk

*to her seems empty and dull? How can I keep my
vow to You?*

Why won't You take these feelings away?

"Doesn't Mom kn-know I'm fine?" Noah's
face contorted in a glower. "She t-treats me like
a b-baby."

"Actually she's treating you like an adult, Noah,"
Rick said. "She asked us to pray for Daniel. They
think he might have caught a very serious disease."

"Oh." His blue eyes narrowed. "Am I g-going
to g-get it?"

"I hope not, but I can't say for sure," Rick explained quietly. "If you get a fever or start to feel
unwell, I'll take you to the hospital right away.
But for tonight your mom wants you to stay here.
Okay?"

Noah nodded. "W-will she b-be okay?" he asked,
uncertainty lacing his voice.

"Let's ask God to protect her," Rick said. But
though he prayed as hard as he could, he felt as if
his prayers simply bounced off the thick barriers
between him and God.

Later, when Noah was asleep, words that Cassie's
father had once spoken to him returned, a strong
admonition he'd given after Rick had asked for his
help to get into the ministry.

"Don't make any vows you can't keep, son. If
you're going to promise God to do His work, to
let Him use you, you'd better be prepared to deny
yourself. Keeping your promises could cost far
more than you ever imagined."

For the very first time since he'd accepted Christ as his Savior, Rick regretted his promise to remain single. Worse than that, doubts about God's purpose for him had taken root. Maybe he wasn't supposed to be in Churchill.

You don't deserve her. How could she ever love you, the man responsible for the childhood she spent without a father? The man who cost her father his precious savings, savings that could have helped her when she was desperate for help?

This is the payment to be exacted for your greed.

Rick was willing to pay, to give up every dream he'd ever dreamed, if that was what God wanted, if it would help Cassie. But how was he to stop the sweet burst of joy that filled his heart whenever he saw her face? How was he to ignore the rush of love that burst inside like fireworks when she laughed or said his name or asked his help?

Love?

His heart stopped as the knowledge flowed through every cell of his body.

He loved Cassie Crockett.

Strong and beautiful, sweet and giving, Cassie was altogether lovely, in spirit and in action. She was everything he'd imagined a woman he'd love would be, from the moment he'd started seeing her face in his dreams so many years ago, not long after his first glance at her picture on her father's desk. It was Cassie's face he'd used as a model whenever he'd dreamed of being loved. Though he hadn't known her then, it was her he imagined by his side.

Now, knowing Cassie, Rick could imagine a future brimming with joy and love, caring and giving.

And yet...

He'd made a vow. That vow meant Cassie—precious, beloved Cassie—could never be his, no matter how much his heart longed for her. All the glorious possibilities Rick had glimpsed through the years shrank and faded away as he sat shrouded in darkness and faced the truth of his future.

There could be no love to finally fill that vacant spot inside him. No wife, no family to protect and plan for, no chance to nurture and love. He could have none of that because he owed a debt.

Hours passed as Rick struggled to surrender the love that beckoned him to forsake his faith and follow his heart. Finally, aching and empty, he let go of it all.

Your will, God. I will do Your will.

Chapter Twelve

"Daniel's going to be fine. It isn't meningitis, it's a virulent flu," Cassie told Rick over the phone.

The reassuring knowledge that Rick was there to listen, to care, to help, sent sweet joy to her heart. How she treasured the bond of sharing with him.

"Thank God," he said, and she knew he meant it.

"Yes. We've seen a lot more cases come in through the night, however. Did you get your flu shot this year, Rick?"

"I did."

Cassie paused, seeing his face in her mind. Precious face, precious man. "How's Noah?"

"He's fine," Rick assured her. "School has been canceled so he's working here."

"He had his flu shot last fall so it's fine for you to take him back to Lives. Apparently, Daniel was the only one of the boys who hadn't had it." A flush of warmth suffused her. "I can't thank you enough for stepping in last night. I appreciate all you've done for Noah."

"No problem." Rick paused then asked, "When will you finish there?"

"Not for a while. This virus has taken out a lot of staff. I'm filling in where they need me. It's been crazy busy." She stopped to yawn. "I'm going to grab a couple hours of sleep here and then I'll get back on duty."

"Is there anything I can do?" he asked.

The words were kind, but Cassie heard distance in Rick's voice. Maybe he was tired of having a kid around, especially a cranky, grumpy one.

And yet, she couldn't quite make herself believe that was the reason. She'd been hearing the distance in his voice on and off for a while now.

"Cassie?"

"Sorry, I zoned out for a minute." She got her brain in gear. "You could get the boys to check on your elderly parishioners. This virus hits seniors very hard. The sooner they come in to the hospital, the better."

"Good idea. Noah and I will pick up the others if Laurel agrees. How are *you* holding up, Cassie?"

"A little rest and I'll get my second wind back." She hesitated. "How did you fare after a night with my son?"

"Actually, it was fun." His voice dropped. Cassie figured Noah must be nearby. "We played some games after dinner. He beat me, as usual."

"It was a lot easier to do my job knowing you

were there for him," she said. "Thank you for being such a good friend."

Would Rick hear in her words how much *more* she wanted than friendship?

"You're welcome. Now is there anything I can do for you personally?" The briskness of Rick's voice was at odds with what he was asking. "Anything?" he repeated.

"If I phoned Laurel and asked her to pack a bag, could you pick it up when you get the boys and drop it here on your way past?" Cassie asked after a moment's thought.

Rick agreed and then quickly got off the phone. Cassie worried that maybe by asking him to care for Noah, she'd asked too much. And yet, Rick loved kids. He'd become a pro at coaxing Noah out of whatever mood he was in. No, something else was bothering him.

And Cassie now felt sure it was whatever he'd been trying to tell her about for a while now, but never quite managed to say.

Confused, Cassie went to sprawl on a cot in the staff room. Too tired to puzzle it out, she finally closed her eyes and let sleep claim her.

But it wasn't the restorative sleep Cassie needed. Instead, she dreamed of the handsome preacher. Though she tried to reach him, he kept backing away, insisting he couldn't care for her, that she wasn't the kind of woman he needed for a wife. She hadn't helped her husband through his crisis, nor was she having success with her son. She was a failure.

Cassie woke feeling as if a gray cloud hung over her. She couldn't shake the disquieting thought that trusting Rick so completely was a mistake.

She rose and went down to the cafeteria for a cup of coffee and something to eat before she went back to work. Thanks to the odd dream she'd had, she felt strangely subdued when Rick entered, carrying a small bag.

"I brought your things. What is *that?*" he asked, looking askance at the half-full bowl in front of her.

"Porridge. Somehow I don't seem to have the energy to eat it," she admitted wearily.

"Leave it. I'll get you some real food." He walked over to the counter, flashed a smile at the woman behind it and soon returned with a fluffy, steaming omelet. "Try that," he said setting it before her.

"The cafeteria doesn't make omelets," Cassie said, unable to stop staring at him as her soul soaked in the beloved lines of his tired face.

"They do today. Eat up. You need some protein." Rick leaned back in his chair, crossed his arms over his chest and raised an eyebrow. "Well?" he demanded when she didn't pick up her fork.

Cassie obediently placed a forkful of the omelet in her mouth. Her eyes widened as the delicious flavors woke up her senses. Rick got up and refilled her coffee cup, and got one for himself. He waited until she'd finished everything on the plate before he spoke again. "Thanks for suggesting we visit the seniors," he said quietly. "We've lost Mr. Saunders but we managed to get help for others who were in trouble."

"I heard about Mr. Saunders," Cassie said. "I'm so sorry."

"Thanks." Rick's chin drooped to his chest, his eyes downcast. "He was an amazing man. His integrity never wavered. What he said, he did." Rick said the words slowly, thoughtfully.

That feeling that something was going on with him, something she didn't understand, nagged at Cassie.

"I hope people remember me as fondly as everyone speaks of him." Touched by Rick's dejection, Cassie reached out to rest her hand on his shoulder to express her sympathy. He didn't immediately pull away. For a moment, the pastor leaned into her touch, as if he needed it to deal with his sorrow.

But a moment later Rick drew back. He lifted his head to look at her and Cassie realized something had changed in their relationship. Something had come between them.

"What's wrong?" she whispered as fear built inside. "You can tell me, Rick. In fact, I think you've been trying to tell me for some time now."

He looked directly at her. "You've been a good friend, Cassie."

Emphasis on *friend*. She'd been right. He was distancing himself. But why?

"And you've been a good friend to me," she said very quietly. "What's bothering you, Rick? Can I help?"

"Now *you* want to help *me?*" Rick gave a soft chuckle. "Don't you have enough to do, woman? You're working overtime, you're dead tired and you want to help me?"

"If I can." She held his gaze and her breath, waiting.

"You're quite a lady, Cassie Crockett." Respect laced his voice. She also thought she heard a note of caring in his kind words. But if he did, why was he trying so hard to build distance between them?

She wanted so much to help him, to give back just a bit of the help he'd so unstintingly offered her. But more than that, she wanted to share the burden of whatever troubles made his shoulders bow.

Most of all, she wanted to love him, and have him love her.

Love. I love him.

For a moment that knowledge paralyzed Cassie. All she could do was stare at him, filling her senses with his presence, letting the rush of joy suffuse her body.

She loved him. But he was hurting.

"Please let me help you," she whispered.

Rick gazed at her. The pure emerald-green of his eyes laid bare his emotions—sadness, grief, helplessness, but worst of all a despondency Cassie had never seen in him before.

"I can't."

Stung, Cassie drew back.

"I need to tell you something," he said, his voice raw, ragged, as if he was having trouble breathing. "Something important."

Her pager went off. Cassie wanted to scream at the interruption. She needed to know what was wrong between them so she could fix it.

"I'm sorry," she said, rising slowly.

"I know." Rick rose, too, carrying her bag. "I'll leave this at the desk for you. You can pick it up later."

"Thank you." She couldn't make herself go, couldn't leave him like this. The pager went off a second time. "Rick, let's make sure we talk later, okay?"

"Take care of yourself, Cassie," Rick said, his voice hoarse and strained.

Why did it sound as if he was saying goodbye?

Aching for the pain he seemed to be in, Cassie stood on tiptoe and pressed a kiss against his cheek.

"You take care of yourself, too, Rick," she said, then hurried away with no understanding of what had just happened between them.

Lord? I trust You. Please help him.

Cassie halted, and took a moment to amend her prayer.

Please help us.

For seven long days the flu epidemic raged through Churchill. Rick drove himself to be the pastor his community needed. He prayed by parishioners' bedsides through long, lonely nights and worry-filled days. He fetched and carried whenever he was asked. He drove countless people to the hospital. He made sure those who were fighting the flu at home had all they needed.

He made himself as useful as he could around Lives, too. He and Teddy Stonechild helped Laurel take care of the boys' meals so Sara could stay home and keep her baby safe.

In a way, the long nights and wearying days were a panacea, allowing Rick to avoid the painful acceptance of what he knew God was asking him to give up—what he now accepted as a soul-deep love for Cassie. He told himself he kept up his frenetic pace because his job was to minister to people.

But that wasn't the whole truth.

As day after weary day passed, each time he caught a glimpse of Cassie in the hospital, all thoughts of his ministry fled. The vibrancy that had always characterized her bouncing gold curls and melting brown eyes faded. Her beautiful face grew thin and drawn as she lost weight from working so hard. The only thing that cheered Rick was seeing her never-faltering smile that was always at the ready for patients and staff alike. When she smiled at *him,* he wished for the privilege of seeing it every day for the rest of his life.

But Rick knew that could never be. No one could wreak the kind of pain and havoc he had and get away scot-free.

She smiled at him now, as she sat across from him in their now-familiar meeting spot in the cafeteria. He could hear the harshness in his own voice and knew concern underlay it.

"You need to get out of here," he said, hating how pale she was, and worried by the way her hand trembled when she lifted her coffee cup.

"A few more hours," she murmured, closing her eyes to savor the brew. "Fresh staff will arrive then and I'll be able to leave."

"Can you last that long?" He struggled to stem his irritation at whoever had asked her to keep working when she was obviously so exhausted.

"Oh, Rick, how can you ask that?" She shook her head at him and for a moment her lovely brown eyes sparkled with a hint of mischief. "Don't you know 'I can do all things through Christ who strengthens me'?"

He had to smile. In spite of all the difficulty she'd endured, or perhaps because of it, Cassie's faith had grown by leaps and bounds this week. He'd overheard her quoting an encouraging verse to another staff member. She'd even told him yesterday that seeing the precariousness of life had made her realize she needed to keep her faith strong. For that Rick gave praise.

"I'm not the only one who's overworked," she said. "You've been run off your feet looking after everyone, haven't you?" Her big brown eyes peeked through the stray strands of blond curls that tumbled onto her forehead. "I hope you're taking care of yourself."

"Don't worry about me." Rick had made up his mind that today, he would finally tell her what he'd done to her father. And yet as he sat here, looking at her, feeling what he felt for her, he realized he couldn't do it.

The knowledge shook him to the core. How could he be so weak, so selfish?

"I *do* worry about you, Rick." Cassie's eyes sent his a silent message that made his skin hum. His fingers itched to push that tendril of gold off her face. "I'm going to go finish my shift." She stood and looked at him for a moment longer, clearly giving him an opportunity to say something more. When he didn't, she gave him a tired smile and turned.

"I'll talk to you later," he called to her.

She waved a hand and kept going.

Rick left the hospital moments later. He needed to pray for strength to tell the truth. The fact that he had been tempted to keep quiet, to let the silence about his past continue, was unbearable.

Because he now realized that Cassie cared for him. The look in her eyes, the way she'd touched him—suddenly everything was clear. She felt about him the same way he felt about her.

Not my will, but Thine, he repeated in his mind over and over again, feeling his heart crack as he drove to the church.

* * *

Cassie stood outside the hospital and drew the frosty March air into her lungs. It felt so good to finally escape the sickness and loss, to let the sunshine warm her skin.

She saw a dark-haired man bend to lift a child from a car and her heart stopped. Rick. She opened her mouth to call out, then realized it wasn't him at all.

She laughed out loud. Rick was so much a part of her, in her mind and her heart, that she thought of him constantly. Those moments in the cafeteria—when she'd finally realized that she loved Rick as she'd never loved before—had been the start of exploring a new vision of what her future could be, a future that she'd never dreamed was possible.

Rick filled her mind and her senses, her dreams and her waking moments. He was everything a man should be: strong without being overbearing, gentle but firm when necessary, caring, committed, thoughtful. The list could go on and she'd never fully describe the man who'd come to mean the world to her.

And he cared about Noah.

Thank You for giving me this love, she prayed as she walked toward her car in the staff parking lot. *Please help me now.*

She needed help because she was going to tell Rick how she felt. She was going to bare her heart to him and trust that he returned her love, that God would work it out.

Cassie kept a steady stream of prayers flowing as she unplugged her car's block heater, then sat inside and waited for the engine to warm up. Doubts crept in, making her wonder if today was the right day, if this was the right time, if Rick would reject her. But Cassie resolutely pushed away her uncertainties and recited verses she'd memorized, verses designed to build her trust in God.

As she did, an idea flickered through her mind. So often she asked God for things, just as Noah often asked her. Before the flu epidemic, he'd pestered her about taking boxing lessons. Cassie had staunchly refused. She'd attended a boxing match once with Eric and had been appalled, so she'd remained adamantly against her son being subjected to such violence.

Did God feel the same when He refused things His children pleaded for, things He knew would be detrimental to them? He was her heavenly Father, He loved and cared for her. Sometimes He said no to her requests because He knew what was best.

Wouldn't God, like any other parent, appreciate being thanked?

Enter into His gates with thanksgiving and a thanks offering, and into His courts with praise! Be thankful and say so to Him, bless and affectionately praise His name.

When was the last time she'd thanked God for anything?

With a grimace, Cassie shoved a CD in the player and let the heart-lifting melodies soak in. After ten minutes, immensely cheered by her private worship service and with the car giving off a toasty heat, she pulled out of her parking spot.

As she drove to Rick's home, she couldn't help noticing the brilliance of the sun. The days were longer now. Easter was just two weeks away. She wondered how the choir and band were doing. Rick had said nothing about practice, probably because he didn't want to worry her when she was so involved with her patients. But Noah had told her during their daily phone call that the group kept practicing.

Singing was the one thing she and Noah could consistently talk about without arguing.

Cassie's mood continued to lift the closer she got to Rick's house. It stood isolated, alone on the cliff top at the end of the street. His car was there, as well as his snowmobile, so she knew he was home.

The full realization of what she was about to do—bare her heart to this man she'd come to trust—made her pulse thrum with excitement and hope. She pulled into his drive and parked her car.

This was it.

"Be with me, Lord," she murmured as she walked over the snow, footsteps crunching loudly in the silence of the afternoon. "Soon Rick will know how much I care for him. Please, please let him love me back." She inhaled then pressed the doorbell.

There was a long delay. Cassie was about to press it a second time when the door was suddenly flung open.

Cassie stared at her son, standing there in some kind of unfamiliar workout clothes with boxing gloves on his hands and a helmet covering his head. She stepped inside and pushed the door closed behind her, frowning.

"Noah? What are you doing?"

"B-boxing with R-Rick." She could hear the challenge in his voice as he told her, "We p-practice lots. Rick s-says I'm g-getting g-good."

"Who is it, Noah?" Rick appeared behind her son, also wearing gloves. His welcoming smile bloomed when he saw Cassie. "Hi."

She ignored the greeting.

"You're teaching my son to box?" she asked in disbelief. He nodded as if it were a perfectly normal thing to do. "Why?"

"Because he asked me to." Rick motioned to a chair. "Do you want to sit down? It won't take a minute for him to change."

"No, I don't want to sit down." Cassie blazed inside. "How could you do this, Rick?"

He blinked, confusion clouding his eyes. "I don't understand—"

Furious with him, Cassie turned to her son. "What I want to know is why you specifically disobeyed me, Noah." She held his defiant gaze. "I refused when you asked me the first time and I kept on refusing," she reminded. "I know you heard me. So why?"

"Cassie, I didn't know you'd forbidden it," Rick interrupted. "I'm truly sorry. I had no idea I was going against your wishes."

"But you didn't bother to ask my permission, either, did you? The first time you ever mentioned boxing to Noah, I know you could see that I didn't like the idea." That same old wall of distrust began building inside, brick by impenetrable brick. "You should have asked me," she said.

"D-don't blame R-Rick!" Noah shouted.

She stared at him, shocked by the fury he directed at her.

"I n-need to d-defend myself." Scorn filled his bitter words. "Y-You turned your b-back on m-me and everyone else. You c-closed down instead of f-fighting for what you b-believe. I'm n-not g-going to be l-like you, M-Mom."

"How can you say that?" Bewildered, Cassie could only stare at the son she would gladly give her life for. "Your father—"

"D-dad would n-never have let people diss us l-like you d-did. You g-gave them b-back their m-money, but they k-kept on s-saying we s-stole it and y-you l-let them. You d-didn't s-stand up for us. Y-You didn't s-stand up for *me*." Tears welled but he dashed them away angrily. "Y-you didn't even n-notice what I w-was going through."

"That's not true."

"I think we're finally learning what's been bothering Noah for so long," Rick said in a very gentle tone. His arm slid around her shoulder as if to impart strength. Cassie, confused and brimming with suspicion, tried to pull away. But Rick drew her to a chair and urged her into it.

"Listen," he urged in a whisper. "He needs to say this."

Cassie could not tear her gaze from his. The tenderness she saw there was a balm to her injured heart. She stared into his green eyes, her confusion growing. Had she been wrong to trust this man? *No,* her heart whispered. Rick would help her, whatever was wrong. Somehow she knew that one thing was true in spite of the doubts that flooded in.

Finally she nodded.

"You have the floor, Noah." Cassie saw something unspoken flow between them. "Get it off your chest, but when you're finished, you're going to listen to what your mother has to say."

Noah drew in a deep breath, then turned to her. In unforgiving, bitter language he blamed her for everything that had happened since his father's death. "I w-was the school f-fool," he said, his tone blistering. "My f-friends c-called me n-names, said I w-was a crook. They s-said we were u-using the church's m-money."

"We weren't," she said, unable to remain totally silent under the assault.

"I d-didn't know th-that. All I knew was that w-we didn't g-go to ch-church anymore," Noah said in a cold, hard tone. "Y-you were always w-working. I h-had nobody t-to talk to when it g-got r-really bad. N-nobody believed m-me when I s-said we didn't t-take the m-money." His face tightened. "Th-they would h-have believed y-you. B-but you w-wouldn't s-say anything. I g-got b-beat up b-because you w-wouldn't t-tell the t-truth."

A part of Cassie was nearly ecstatic that Noah was finally talking. She prayed that he would finally find healing. Another part of her reeled at his accusations. But as he spoke, her son's blame, his censure and most of all his feeling of being alone gutted her. All she could do was listen.

At last Noah finished, pale but still defiant. Cassie couldn't speak.

"So because you were mad at your mother, because you blamed her for the pain you suffered when your dad died, because you needed to feel strong and invincible, that's why you started picking fights?" Rick said.

Noah bowed his head.

"Picking fights?" Cassie said, her voice raw. "Noah was bullied."

"No." Rick shook his head. "Tell her, Noah." When Noah didn't respond, Rick continued. "You deliberately picked on other kids, pushing them around until they couldn't take it anymore and they hit you. Isn't that true?" Rick asked. After a long pause, the boy nodded. "You lashed out to get rid of the hurt and in doing so, you hurt other people."

Cassie saw the truth of Rick's accusations on Noah's face.

"H-how d-did you know?" Noah mumbled.

"It was just a hunch, something you said the day you gave me a nosebleed."

"He gave you a—" Cassie began.

Rick cut her off, his focus on Noah. "Thank you for admitting the truth, Noah."

"I feel like I don't know you at all," Cassie whispered, aghast at what she was hearing.

"You don't know m-me," Noah growled.

Rick's glower marred his handsome face. "I'm not sure I do, either. You conned me into teaching you boxing because you needed a way to get the upper hand with kids who wouldn't back down from your threats."

"Yes." The admission hissed from Noah's lips.

"The thing is, I never realized your mother had forbidden it." Rick's voice was hard. "I don't like being used, Noah. I especially don't like being used against your mother."

"I'm s-sorry," Noah said without remorse.

"Are you?" Rick held his gaze. "You had lots to say about the people in your former church and how they treated you so miserably. You accused your mother of not standing up to them." Rick's severe tone held Noah captive.

"Sh-she didn't," Noah sputtered.

"No, she didn't, because your mother is the strongest woman I've ever known. She stood tall, did what she could to make amends for your dad's mistake and then picked up and moved here to help *you*." Rick shook his head when Noah tried to argue. "I think *you're* the one who isn't standing up to the problem. Instead of facing the issues and dealing with them, you're hiding behind anger." Rick's tone softened. "You hurt kids who only wanted to be friends with you, Noah. You did to them exactly what people did to you. You've got a lot of burned bridges to repair if you want to have real friends here."

Cassie could stay silent no longer. "I'm not sure I understand everything you're saying, Rick." She frowned at him. "But I wish you'd come to me with what you suspected about Noah. I feel like you've kept things hidden from me."

Rick met her gaze and held it. "I'm sorry. I wanted to wait until you were more rested before I opened this wound. Now that everything's come to light, I'm sure Noah can clear up any questions you have."

"I have quite a few." She looked at her son. "You've made a lot of assumptions about me. You judged me and condemned me, but whether you believe it or not, everything I've done has been for you." When Noah had no response, she said, "We'll talk at home. Get your things and let's go."

"Cassie, I'm sorry—"

"Not now, Rick." Cassie waited while Noah pulled sweatpants and a shirt over his training clothes. She couldn't shed her feelings of betrayal—Rick should have told her, should have clued her in. "Let's go, Noah."

Rick walked them to the door. When Cassie looked into his eyes, she could think of nothing to say. Finally, she stepped outside into the snow, leaving Rick behind her as she wondered how everything had gone so horribly wrong.

She'd come over here to tell Rick she was in love with him. And now here she was, feeling betrayed, crushed, heartbroken.

How quickly things could change and fall apart.

What a fool she'd been.

Chapter Thirteen

Cassie had been gone all of two minutes when Rick grabbed his keys and dashed out the door to his car. He'd put off talking to her for so long now it was embarrassing. What kind of man hides from the truth the way he'd been hiding? And he called himself a pastor?

His heart was pounding as he drove to Lives. He was driving too fast, recklessly even. At the rate he was going, he'd probably get there before her, if he didn't end up crashing his car.

Breathe, he told himself. *You're almost there. The truth is almost out. Just breathe.*

When he pulled into the driveway, Cassie and Noah were about to go inside. Cassie nodded at her son as if to tell Noah to go ahead without her, and then she waited, arms crossed, for Rick to approach.

And when he did, she gave him a piece of her mind.

"I trusted you," she said quietly. "I let go of all

my inhibitions and I put my faith in you because I was certain you had our best interests at heart."

"I do," he said, chagrin under his quiet words.

"Do you?" she asked. There was a hard edge to her voice that Rick had never heard before. "It doesn't feel like you do when you're keeping Noah's deceit to yourself."

"I didn't know it was deceit! But I was going to talk to you. I was waiting for the right time—"

"I was, too," she whispered. "Do you know why I came to see you today, Rick? I was going to tell you that I thought we had something special between us. Now I'm wondering. I want so badly to trust you. I'm trying to trust you but you keep putting this distance between us."

Rick couldn't deny it, and he offered no defense. With a heavy sigh, Cassie turned to go inside. He gripped her arm, halting her movement.

She turned, frowning at his hand on her arm, and said. "I feel like I don't know you or Noah."

"You *don't* know me, Cassie. You shouldn't trust me because I don't deserve it." Just saying those words made him feel lighter. He was getting closer. Closer to telling her everything.

"Why?" she asked, hesitantly.

It was time.

"Cassie, I am a much bigger cause of the trouble between you and father than you realize. Because of me, your father lost…everything. He lost his life savings, and money he had put aside for you and

Noah. I'm the reason he couldn't help you when you needed him most."

Cassie's face registered many emotions as she processed what Rick had just told her, but all she said was "Tell me."

Rick took a deep breath, air rushing into his lungs for what felt like the first time in months. "You know I grew up on the streets," he began. "I was alone. Until I met your dad."

"You told me about that."

"John helped me graduate from high school, and he helped me get a scholarship to go to college where I majored in finance. I became a stockbroker. I was good at it. I took risks and they paid off. Hugely." The irony of it all washed over him once again. "I had money enough for two lifetimes. I should have been satisfied, but taking risks became a game to me—how far could I go? The more risks I took, the wealthier my clients got and the more I needed to risk to get the high I craved. I was the golden boy of brokers." He paused a moment, remembering those heady days with chagrin.

"What did you do to my father?" Cassie's voice snapped him back to the present.

He stared at her, his soul dark with guilt. "One of my clients was a publisher. I made him very wealthy with some high-risk investments. That gave him the idea to publish a series on high-risk, high-return investing for do-it-yourself investors. He asked me to write one book in a series he was publishing. My topic was risk-taking in the market." Rick ran a hand through his hair as he tried to figure out how to continue.

"Okay." She stared at him in confusion.

"It was a game to me, Cassie, a way to show off. I included every risky maneuver I'd ever tried in it and some new ones I was trying on my clients just so I could write about them. My name wasn't on the cover, so I thought, where's the risk?" He shook his head.

Cassie sat silent, her eyes widening with every word.

"I used your father's money for the riskiest move I ever made because I wanted to repay him for everything he'd done for me. His account built like crazy and I figured my approach was paying off. I put it in the book and it sold like crazy."

Cassie's face said everything he knew she was thinking. If he was so wealthy, what was he doing here in Churchill, living in a dinky house, having to sell his guitar to raise funds for Michael's saxophone?

"I'm sorry but I don't see—"

"I thought I was invincible and I took one gamble too many," he said, hating the words even as he said them. Guilt crushed him over the pain he'd caused with his arrogance. "I lost everything I owned and everything my clients had entrusted to me. I had a fiancée at the time—I lost her family's benevolent fund." Rick swallowed. "And I lost the money your father had spent a lifetime saving."

He waited as moments passed and his words sank in. Horror filled Cassie's face.

"That's why he wouldn't help me," she said, understanding dawning.

"Yes. Because he couldn't. Because of me. Because of my greed." Rick felt sick at the words. But he plowed on, desperate to confess everything. "Overnight I went from top of the heap to the bottom. I became the investment guru brought down by his own folly. I was a laughingstock. My friends didn't know me anymore. The woman I loved left me."

"I'm sorry, Rick." Cassie's brown eyes shone with tears.

"Don't be sorry for me, Cassie," he ordered, angered by her tender response. "I got exactly what I deserved. I was showing off, showing them all that a kid from the street could beat the rich folks at their own game." *Oh, Lord, forgive me for my pride.* "I used other people's life savings to get approval and acceptance. I cost families their homes, their futures. For God's sake, don't feel sorry for me."

The sadness on Cassie's face—the tenderness—remained. It was almost more than Rick could bear.

"The worst thing is, *I* deserved to lose everything, but they didn't. Your father didn't. They all trusted me and I abused that trust."

"You don't have to tell me this, Rick. It's none of my business," Cassie whispered.

"Yes, it is! You're one of the people I hurt with

my greed. My actions caused irreparable damage in your life and for that I am profoundly sorry." Rick swallowed.

"What did my father do?" Cassie asked gently.

"I'd decided to end my life when your dad found me. He should have hated me for what I'd done to him." The wonder of it was as profound now as it had been when it first happened. "Instead, your father helped me sober up. Then he told me that even though I'd made such a colossal mess of my life, God still had plans for me, good plans. I stayed with him and he helped me get straightened out. Every day he taught me about God. And when I decided I wanted to commit my life to Him, your father helped me get into seminary."

"I'm glad he was there for you," she said simply. There was no regret in her voice, no blame.

There should have been.

"The day I was ordained, I made a promise to God." Rick summoned his courage—this was the last thing he had to confess to the beautiful woman standing in front of him, her gorgeous face radiating compassion he didn't deserve.

"Say it, Rick," she whispered.

"I knew I could never make up for the lives I'd ruined. So I made a vow to give up my dreams and goals and dedicate my entire life to His cause." He lifted his head and looked directly into Cassie's eyes. "That's why I've gotten so involved at Lives. Your dad helped me understand that my showboating, my high-living, my risk-taking was all a plea for someone to love me, to see past the kid who'd lived in the gutter and accept me as worthy of love. I was trying to fill a hole in my heart that no one but God could fill."

She nodded as if she understood.

"That's why I work with the boys at Lives," he said quietly. "I want them to know that no matter how bad it was, no matter what they did, they are loved, that I am there for them always."

"The boys know that," she said gently, her eyes shining.

"I hope so." He struggled to resist the urge to reach for her, to pull her into his arms. He would never have the right to do that again. "I'm very touched that you care for me, Cassie. But you can't waste your love on me. I promised God I'd atone for my guilt by giving up the one thing I've always longed for—a family of my own, someone to love. Someone who loves me."

Cassie was silent for a very long time, studying him. He held her gaze, forcing himself to stand up to her scrutiny. "You're saying that you're trying to make up for your mistakes by never letting yourself love, is that it?"

In the depths of her brown eyes, Rick could suddenly see unfathomable pain. "So instead of filling that empty spot in your soul with money, now you're going to fill it with duty."

"If you want to put it that way."

"Tell me something, Rick. Do you love me?"

The words crashed over him like a tidal wave.

Every fiber of his being wanted to tell her *yes.* "It doesn't matter," he said.

"It does to me. Answer the question."

He knew that he owed her the truth, as painful as it was to admit. "Yes, Cassie, I do." He watched as her eyes filled with tears. "But nothing can come of it. I'm in debt to God," Rick said somberly.

"A debt of love, which you are trying to repay with sacrifice," she murmured.

"Cassie, I don't deserve to love and be loved. Keeping my vow is the only way I know to atone for what I've done." He raked a hand through his hair, wishing he could make her understand.

She simply looked at him.

"I wish I could erase it all. I wish I could be the man you need, the man you think you love. But even if I could, what I've done would always stand between us." Rick desperately craved the sound of her voice, her touch on his hand, something. But she remained still and silent. "I have to keep my vow. That's why there can never be anything between us. I'm sorry, Cassie."

"So am I, Rick." With one last look at him, Cassie silently turned and disappeared inside Lives.

Rick stood there a moment, stunned by the overwhelming waves of loss that swamped him. He ached to hold this woman he'd come to love. He hadn't meant to love her, but it had happened because he'd lost sight of his promise. Once again he'd failed God.

In that moment, Rick knew the time had come to leave Churchill.

His spirit felt lost, cast adrift, decimated at the thought of never again seeing Cassie and Noah.

Lord? Where are you? Help me, please. No response. Had God abandoned him because he'd forgotten his vow?

After Easter, after the kids had presented their cantata, he'd leave this place he'd come to love, this place that seemed like home.

And once he was away from here, maybe Rick could find a way to end this desperate need to have Cassie in his arms, in his heart, in his life.

Cassie entered Lives feeling as if she'd been knocked to the ground not once but twice. First Noah's demoralizing tirade had rocked her world. Then Rick's bombshell explanation that his love for her could never be realized had doused the joy she'd reveled in earlier. Life had seemed full of possibilities this morning—now it seemed empty.

Noah stood waiting in the hall.

"My room," she said to him quietly. "You and I are going to talk."

Noah shot her a dark look, but did as she asked. Cassie closed the door, suddenly overwhelmed. Tears that could not be suppressed rose in a great tide of sadness and she let them fall, unable to stem her sobs. "Mom?" Noah gazed at her uncertainly. "D-don't cry, Mom."

The tears kept flowing. "All I wanted when I

decided to move us here was for you to be happy. But you're not. I've done everything wrong."

"No, y-you haven't," he said.

"Then how do you explain the fact that you've been hurting other people intentionally, Noah?" she demanded, dashing away the tears from her cheeks. "The worst thing is, you hurt them to make yourself feel better. Do you realize you could be sent to jail, just like the boys at Lives have?"

"It's m-my fault." Noah closed his eyes. "I kn-know it d-doesn't h-help now, b-but I'm r-really sorry, Mom."

"Why are you sorry?" she demanded, afraid to believe in him.

"I d-didn't realize what I was doing t-to you and to R-Rick." Shame suffused his face and he looked down at the floor. "I n-never meant t-to hurt him. I n-never realized—" He choked up. Several moments passed before he could speak again. "H-He's always been g-good to me. I d-didn't think—"

"That's the thing, isn't it?" Cassie said. "You didn't think how your actions would affect Rick or anyone else, including me."

"Y-You?" He frowned.

"Think about it. What happens if you get into trouble? Do you think the government will want the mother of a kid with a criminal record working with troubled kids?"

Shock covered his face. "I d-didn't—"

"Think that far ahead? Everything we do in this life has ramifications, Noah. You throw a stone and the ripples spread out far and wide." She closed her eyes. "I thought you were mature enough to realize that, especially after what happened when your father died. I guess I was wrong."

Noah sat down on the side of the bed as if a heavy responsibility weighed him down. "I'm s-so sorry," he whispered. "I was angry b-because you didn't treat me like the m-man of the family, but I d-don't deserve that. I was s-stupid."

"Nobody gets everything they want in life," Cassie said, the sourness she felt inside tingeing her voice. "We all have to deal with hard things."

"L-like you l-loving Rick?" he asked very quietly.

"What do you know about that?" she asked him, startled.

"I can see it wh-when you look at him," Noah said in a soft tone. "And when he l-looks at you."

"Well, you don't have to worry about it now, Noah," she said, pressing down the surge of sadness as she accepted the truth. "Nothing's going to change."

"Because Rick m-made a vow," Noah said with a nod. "He t-told me about it. He s-said he has to pay for his p-past. I think th-that's wrong."

"Wrong?" Cassie frowned at him. "What do you mean?"

"Rick's always t-talking about f-forgiveness, how God forgives our s-sins and remembers them n-no more. He s-said that's what Easter's all a-about."

He shrugged. "If G-God doesn't r-remember them, why would He w-want Rick to pay for them?"

Cassie stared at him, stung by the wisdom in the words that had come out of her young son's mouth. A smile took over her face and she tentatively put an arm around him. For the first time in a long time, he didn't flinch away.

"That is an excellent question, Noah."

A question Pastor Rick should have to answer.

His last days in Churchill slipped away from Rick like a skate blade across the glinting ice of Hudson Bay. Though it was late March, he found the still-wintry days dreary as he never had before.

He'd replayed his last conversation with Cassie a hundred times, but no matter how he wished otherwise, he'd had no choice. He'd had to push her away, even though it had cost him dearly. What puzzled him was that Cassie seemed to hold no grudge. She'd never said anything about that day when she came to the church on Sundays with Noah, or to choir practice.

Rick hadn't asked her to continue playing for them. She'd simply appeared and waited for his cue. It seemed to him that the kids were suddenly hitting each note exactly as he'd hoped, that they raised their voices in praise and worship as if they now fully grasped the meaning of Easter. For that he was grateful.

But rehearsal was bittersweet torture to Rick as he counted down each precious moment he had left with Cassie. He repeatedly reminded himself that God had brought him here, but that didn't mean God had brought him to Churchill to be with Cassie. It puzzled Rick that God would intentionally put him on this course when He knew Rick would fall for her. But at the same time, the joy he found in seeing her beautiful smile, in hearing her encourage the kids, in sharing a glance that said she still cared for him—that left him breathless.

He wouldn't have traded those moments for the world.

And yet always, always, he faced the knowledge that he must leave here, leave her. Cassie's life would go on. She'd find someone else to love, to share her future with. She was too special for some other guy not to notice her. He wanted that for her.

But he would be alone. It was the way it had to be.

"Are you g-going to see Rick?" Noah asked, staring at Kyle.

"Yeah. He seems down lately." Kyle gave him a grin and grabbed the door.

"Wait. I need to t-tell you something." Noah summoned his courage. He had to fix things. "Rick l-loves my mom, you know."

"I kind of guessed." Kyle frowned. 'How does your mom feel?"

"She loves h-him, too, but Rick did something that hurt my g-grandpa." Noah felt his face get hot, but he didn't stop. "I know I shouldn't have d-done it, but I was listening at his d-door and I heard him m-make a reservation on the t-train. I'm pretty sure h-he thinks the only way to make it better is to leave. I don't want him to d-do that. Nobody d-does." He peered at Kyle through the falling snow. "Can y-you do s-something?"

"I don't know. But I'm going to try." Kyle slapped him on the shoulder. "Thanks for telling me."

"I w-want my m-mom to be happy. She w-won't be if Rick g-goes away."

"Got it." Kyle went inside.

"What were you saying to Kyle?" his mom asked as he climbed into her car.

"Just man t-talk." Noah spent the ride home praying.

"Rick?" Kyle stood in the now-empty sanctuary, peering at him with a puzzled look. "What are you doing?"

"Where is everyone?" Rick glanced around, realizing that while he'd been daydreaming, everyone had left.

"Gone home for dinner. Wanna share a pizza? Sara's at a baby shower." Kyle waited, his frown growing when Rick just stared at him. "You okay?"

The yearning to see Cassie, to hold her and tell her that he'd never love anyone as he loved her— all of it screamed at him to forsake his vow. He could feel the temptation to relinquish his faith, to abandon it and let himself revel in the love he felt for her.

"Thinking about Cassie?" Kyle asked in a knowing tone.

"You know?" Relief filled him. Rick poured out the whole ugly story. "I don't see a way out of this, buddy. I think I have to leave this place."

"Not so fast. I think we need to pray about that decision. How about if I lead off?" Kyle offered.

"I'd like that." He knelt with his friend and recommitted his life to God

Then Kyle insisted it was time to eat.

Rick went with him, but he wasn't hungry. All he could think about was the question that kept rattling through his brain. If loving Cassie was wrong, why didn't God take his feelings away?

Chapter Fourteen

On Good Friday Cassie went to church.

Rick had invited missionaries from Burma to speak in the morning. After sharing a lunch of soup and sandwiches to commemorate the Last Supper, he led them in a solemn foot-washing ceremony.

Cassie's heart swelled with pride for this man of God. She watched him humbly wash the feet of old and young alike, drawing their focus to the meaningful action Jesus had done, knowing he was to die. With tenderness and quiet respect Rick moved through the small group, his eyes glowing as he ministered. When he came to her, Cassie felt a jolt of response to his touch but Rick seemed unaffected as he poured warm water over her feet into the basin.

"'My protection and success come from God alone,'" he murmured as he dried her feet on a towel. "'He is my refuge, a Rock where no enemy can reach me. O my people, trust him all the time. Pour out your longings before him for he can help.'"

His head lifted as he finished speaking and for one timeless moment their eyes met. Cassie saw a tender, gentle love in his gaze. How she ached to respond, to reach out and embrace him, willing him to forget everything but caring for her.

For a moment she thought he would. But then he closed his eyes and, without looking at her again, moved on to the person beside her.

Why God? her soul cried. *He loves me. I know he does. And I love him. Is that wrong?*

"Your will be done," she heard Rick say.

Us loving each other—that's not Your will? Tears slipped between her lashes. *I can't have him, can I?*

A soft rush of certainty filled her. God was saying no. Oh, how that hurt. She took deep breaths then dabbed at the wetness on her cheeks.

God had something for Rick to do, a mission that was more important than loving Cassie Crockett. She couldn't stand in the way of that. Not after she'd seen his extraordinary gift for ministry. His heart was for God and he took his vow seriously. She could not diminish his dedication by asking him to break that vow.

She didn't think she could turn her back on the joy and the rightness of being with him. But as Rick stood in their circle, reminding them of how much God had sacrificed to have each of them as His child, Cassie suddenly understood. She'd finally learned that no matter what happened, God came first. Somehow He would help her give up the desire of her heart if she trusted Him completely.

As one the group rose, joined hands and sang the first verse of the hymn "Old Rugged Cross." Cassie was struck anew by the depth of Rick's abilities. She wasn't the only one with tears drying on her cheeks. Others in the congregation had been as deeply moved and a few, like her, lingered in the sanctuary to absorb or perhaps prolong the glory they'd experienced.

It took a long time to resolve the turmoil in her heart. Part of her longed to ignore God's will, to grab hold of her happiness and hang on, to beg him to give up his vow. She wanted what she wanted.

And yet how much more guilt would Rick feel? Cassie couldn't do that to him. For Rick's sake, she released everything into God's hands. It would cost her dearly when she saw him and heard his voice, and when her heart argued that she had a right to happiness.

But she had a right to nothing. She'd given up the right to run her life the way she wanted when she'd renewed her faith and trusted God.

It had to be complete trust.

She gazed at the mural of the good shepherd on the wall. It had been painted many years before. The colors were faded and worn except for the eyes. Dark brown, gentle and beckoning, she stared into them and at last found the peace she craved.

He's yours, Lord. Soft and tentative, peace flowed over her soul. She wiped away her tears. "Your will," she murmured at last.

She rose and walked to the exit, but earnest

voices stopped her from leaving. Rick was standing in the foyer, talking to George Stern, who looked upset.

"I'm tendering my resignation, George. Effective immediately." Rick's words hit her with a decimating force. "I'll be leaving Churchill Tuesday morning."

The moment she heard the words, Cassie knew two things instantly and with a certainty that filled her soul. First, this was where God wanted Rick. Churchill needed his love and understanding and patience. This town was his ministry.

And, second, he was resigning because of her, because she was causing him to struggle against the vow he'd made. The weight of it almost crushed her.

Rick could not leave. Churchill was where he belonged.

So she'd have to go.

She'd talk to Laurel and resign. They could find someone to replace her.

But who could replace Rick?

Cassie waited until the two men left. Then she made a beeline for her car. Her dad was arriving tomorrow on the train. She'd tell him her decision, she decided as she drove back to Lives. Maybe after they cleared the air once and for all, she and Noah could go back to Toronto and live with him. It wouldn't be easy on Noah, but she knew he'd understand if she told him about Rick's resignation.

She pulled into the yard and took a good look at

what made up Lives Under Construction. But the exterior, the skating rink, the shed—that wasn't the essence of the project. What mattered were the lives inside, boys who needed a man like Rick to guide them into their future.

Your will be done. With resolute determination Cassie left the car and walked into the house. "Laurel?"

"In the kitchen." Her friend greeted her with a smile that quickly faded when she saw Cassie's face. "What?"

"I have to resign, Laurel. Noah and I have to leave." Then, despite her best intentions, she broke down. Weeping, she explained what had happened.

Laurel listened, but she didn't try to talk Cassie out of her plans. Cassie knew that was because Laurel understood that Rick's presence in Churchill was a necessity. Anyone could nurse a sick boy, but not everyone could be the spiritual leader these kids needed to rebuild their lives.

God needed Rick in Churchill, not Cassie.

It was time to go.

"Dad!" Cassie threw her arms around her father's neck and hugged him tightly. "I'm so glad you came."

"Me, too, honey." He squeezed her and brushed a kiss against her hair. "Where's my grandson?"

"Hey, G-grandpa." Noah rolled his eyes at Cassie as the older man hugged him, but he said nothing, clearly happy to be reunited.

Cassie drove them back to Lives, bubbling with excitement as she and her dad caught up. Noah pointed out landmarks. Once they'd arrived, she introduced her father and they gathered to eat lunch. When it was over, the moment she'd been waiting for finally arrived.

"Can we talk, Dad?" she asked.

"It's about time, don't you think? I need to apologize to you for not supporting you enough after Eric's death."

"I understand now why you couldn't." She clutched his hand in hers. "But why didn't you tell me?"

"Shame. Embarrassment. Maybe some anger." He shook his head. "What kind of father doesn't have enough money put aside to help his own daughter? I felt like a failure."

"Because Rick lost your money," she said.

"He told you." John sighed.

"Yes. Dad." She hesitated. "Are you okay?"

"I'm fine, Cassie. I earn a good salary teaching at the seminary. I don't have a lot of expenses and the government sends me a pension check every month. If you need to borrow—"

"No, no. I was going to lend you some." They grinned at each other.

"Rick's a great guy, isn't he?"

"You can say that after what he did?" Cassie said.

"I was mad at him at the time, but I always knew he was a risk taker." He chuckled. "Rick is the son I never had. Just like I've always prayed for you, I've prayed for him for so many years. I believe God sent him to me to help and I tried my best." Her father's eyes narrowed. "Cassie, I've sensed something in your letters. You care for Rick, don't you?"

"I love him." She wasn't afraid to say it anymore. "It's because of Rick that I learned to trust God." She explained about her decision to leave Churchill.

"You'll live with me." John studied her. "How does Rick feel about you?"

Cassie explained her belief that he loved her.

"He gave his resignation—that's why Noah and I have to move. Rick belongs here, Dad. This place is his ministry, just like yours was always in Toronto. I can't let him give it up for me."

"So he's still determined to keep that vow." John's eyes narrowed. "I brought his guitar. I think I'll pay him a visit tomorrow," he said thoughtfully.

"I love you, Dad." She nestled in his arms, praying that somehow God would help her father help Rick.

"It's so good to see you, John." Rick held his office door wide, then embraced the stooped, gray-haired man who seemed to have aged twenty years since he'd last seen him. Obviously the result of losing his life's savings. He pushed the thought aside. "I'm glad you came for Easter. And doubly glad to see this again." He took the guitar from John, glad to feel the weight of the case in his hands again. "I wish Cassie hadn't done it, but I'm glad she did."

"She knows how important that guitar is to your ministry," John said.

Rick asked about mutual friends and the seminary where John still taught classes, even though he was supposed to be retired. Rick tried to dodge John's personal questions. No way did he want to discuss his feelings for his mentor's daughter. But John was as wily as ever.

"I've been thinking a lot about you recently, son." John tented his hands under his chin, his face thoughtful. "The Lord keeps telling me to pray for you so you'll see more clearly."

"See what more clearly?" Rick asked in puzzlement.

"His love." John leaned forward. "Or, more specifically, His forgiveness."

"Have you and Noah been talking?" Rick asked. "He was in here this morning, asking about me questions about God's forgiveness."

"Cassie told me how my grandson was struggling, and how you helped him see the light. I don't know how to thank you for doing that," John said.

"I only did for him what you did for me." Rick leaned back in his chair. "It's about time I started paying back my debt to you."

"There is no debt, Rick." John frowned. "I told you that long ago. I love you like the son I never had. If I helped you, then it was a God-given privilege, not because I wanted payback." He shook his head. "Are you still trying to keep that vow you made to God in seminary?"

Rick had known it was coming. He exhaled. "Yes. It's the only way I know to repay God."

"So you're still trying to buy your salvation."

Rick blinked. "Buy salvation?"

"What else can you call it? You think if you do enough, strive hard enough and help enough kids that you'll be able to repay God." John leaned forward. "I told you then and I'll tell you now. You can't earn forgiveness from our Lord. It doesn't matter what you do or don't do, He's still forgiven you for the mistakes you made."

"But—"

"Isn't that exactly what Easter is about?" The old man smiled. "The day Jesus died, your sins were forgiven. Period. There's no way you can earn or be worthy of that forgiveness. By trying you negate God's sacrifice."

Rick frowned at the words as they began to sink in.

"If we can be worthy of forgiveness, if we can deny ourselves in order to earn it, then Easter doesn't matter, son." John sighed. "I should have said this a long time ago, the day you made that vow, in fact. But I thought—"

"You're saying we shouldn't make vows to God?" Rick asked.

"I'm saying your vow isn't about God. It's about you, about easing your guilt."

"Me?" Rick shook his head, aghast. "No, I'm trying to make up for my mistakes."

"You can't." John tented his fingers, then peered at him. "You're not in control of the world. If you try to be, you make yourself ineffective for God. You're fixated on the past and what you can do to make amends, but God doesn't want your amends or your guilt. He's already forgiven you. Now He wants you to move on, to do the things He has planned for you."

Rick struggled to wrap his mind around what John was saying, but the next sentence drove all thought from his mind.

"My daughter loves you," John said quietly. "She said you told her you feel the same. But you won't act on those feelings, you won't see that God brought you together, because you're too busy trying to make God see how worthy you are."

Stunned by the condemnation, Rick reeled.

"This vow you made—have you ever asked God what He thinks about it?" John asked. "That's the thing about being in the ministry. We have to constantly measure our motives against God's expectations. Easter is about forgiveness for everybody, regardless of what's in their past. There's no mention of earning it or making repayment because we can never atone. And when we try, we hamstring God." John let that sink in for a moment, then rose. "I have to go, Rick. Noah and I are going to go ice fishing. My grandson and I have a lot of catching up to do."

Rick shook hands with the man he'd revered for so long, his mind in turmoil as he watched John leave the church. Alone, he stared at the cross hanging above the altar. He thought of all the people he'd hurt and of the time he'd spent trying to make up for it.

My grace is sufficient for Thee.

What did that mean? That he'd been wrong to make his vow?

"Rick?"

Cassie's quiet voice drew his attention to the back of the church. Love welled in him like an ocean tide as he soaked in her loveliness. Would he ever get over the yearning to wrap his arms around her and hold her close, to protect her and never let her go? "Cassie," he managed to croak.

"I just wanted to tell you something." She fiddled with bright pink gloves that he knew she'd made. That vibrant color personified Cassie—she brought light and life with her wherever she went. "Noah and I are leaving Churchill. On Tuesday. With my dad."

"What?" Feeling sucker punched, Rick stared at her. Her brown eyes glittered with determination. "Why?" he whispered.

"I know you gave your resignation and I know you did it because of me. But you can't leave. This is your mission field, Rick. This is where you belong." Her voice grew stronger as she spoke. "The kids at Lives, Churchill's seniors, the people who live here—they all need you. This is where God sent you. Because He has a purpose for your life here." She smiled.

"If you leave, who will love the kids in your band and choir? They need to be part of something wonderful. Who will make sure the seniors are okay when the next problem hits? Who will show them that God is a God of love? You can't give up your calling here. I won't be responsible for ruining God's plans."

"But—"

"Because of you, I found God again. I understand now that His will comes first and I know that His will is for you to continue to minister here." She stepped forward. Her fingertips skimmed across his face, cupped his cheek and followed the line of his jaw. She touched her forefinger to his lower lip as if to press a kiss there.

Rick nearly lost it. Every good intention, every resolve, even his vow—they nearly caved in under the rush of longing that wailed through him. His instincts urged him to grab hold of her and hang on for dear life.

"I love you with my whole heart, Rick," she whispered, her smile affectionate yet sad. "But I understand that you have your vow, that you need to keep it and you can't do that if I'm here. So I'll leave wishing you God's very best. I'm so thankful that one of the people you helped heal was my son."

"I'm so sorry, Cassie."

"You don't owe me any apologies, Rick. I just want to say one thing more. It's actually something

Noah asked me," she said. "You preach forgiveness. You've repeated it to the boys, to me and to Noah. You say it over and over."

He nodded.

"But if God is a God of forgiveness and second chances, why can't He forgive you for your past? Since when does God expect atonement for what's already been forgiven?"

She gazed at him a moment longer, then turned and walked out of the church, leaving him with her questions ringing in the air.

Rick stood there feeling broken and lost. "I love you, Cassie," he whispered. But his words fell into the emptiness of the sanctuary.

He returned to his office to work on his sermon for tomorrow, Easter Sunday. But there was no joy in his heart. Nor could he find joy in the glorious music the kids made in their afternoon practice. There certainly was no joy in watching Cassie walk out the door after practice without even looking at him.

Easter was all about joy. But all he felt was loss and guilt.

God doesn't want your guilt. John's words echoed inside his head.

Then what does He want?

Chapter Fifteen

"What are you thinking about, honey?"

Cassie was still adjusting to being around her father, and to his kindness. As he put an arm around her shoulder and hugged her close, sharing her wonder at the Easter morning sunrise, she sent up a quick prayer of thanks.

"Isn't it beautiful?" she whispered. The sun's rays made the snow gleam like a diamond, as if in jubilant praise. "I'll miss this place."

And Rick.

"You don't have to leave."

"Yes, I do. Rick's needed here. I can be replaced." She turned her head slightly, letting a smile tug at her lips. "Most women would fight like crazy for the chance to love a guy like him. He's one in a million."

"But?"

"But this place is his calling. How can I interfere in that? How can I ask him to turn his back on something he believes is his duty?" Cassie clapped her hands together. "Let's not talk about it anymore, okay? Let's just enjoy the time we have left here."

So they did. They shared a riotous breakfast with the boys. While Cassie cooked waffles, her dad insisted on frying mounds of bacon. Laurel got carried away whipping cream enough for twenty people, and yet somehow it all disappeared.

Joy filled the air at Lives Under Construction. From time to time the boys paused in their feast to remind each other of something in their choral presentation. Cassie smiled at the syrup that dotted Noah's T-shirt as he joined in the conversation. His stutter was almost gone and the dark clouds of anger had lifted, leaving behind the child who, because of Rick, was finally able to genuinely interact with the Lives' boys.

"You'd better wait till you're at church before you put on your new shirts," she said. Each boy had a brand-new white shirt, black pants and a black bow tie. "We don't want any spots on this performance."

As she laughed and smiled with them, Cassie could only keep Rick out of her thoughts for minutes at a time. The idea of never seeing Rick again, of never hearing his burst of laughter or the music he could coax from his guitar or his amazing voice—

I'm doing the right thing, aren't I, God?
What else could she do?

It took a lot of work to get the kitchen cleaned up and the boys ready to go. Cassie pulled into the packed church lot with only a few moments to spare before the service began. In a way she was relieved that there was no time to chat—she didn't want any awkwardness in her relationship with Rick.

Later she'd think about all they'd shared, all she'd lost. Today she'd concentrate, pour her heart and soul into her accompaniment and make sure Rick and the kids had the best music she knew how to provide.

She'd do it out of love, for him.

Cassie walked into the church. To her surprise, the church burgeoned with flowers. In the entry, a huge basket of fragrant hyacinths welcomed everyone. A dozen pots of pure white Easter lilies with big glossy yellow bows lined the front of the stage. On either side at the front, someone had arranged two massive vases of bright pink tulips.

One glance at her father's face and Cassie knew he'd done it.

"They must have cost you a mint," she said. "But they're beautiful. They remind me of the flowers Mom always got for our church. It really feels like Easter now."

"Then they were worth every penny." He squeezed her hand, then handed her her music bag. "Break a leg, sweetheart."

After whispering much the same thing to Noah, Cassie walked to the front of the church, laid out her music for the choir then began to play a prelude to quiet the congregation. She deliberately chose hymns she'd learned as a child, words that spoke of the resurrection and the life given by God. As the boys filed into the first two rows, silence fell, allowing the music to soar to the ceiling of the small building. Along with the lovely scent of the flowers, a feeling of joy permeated the packed room as Rick walked through the door to the left of the pulpit.

Please bless him. Let him feel Your presence today.

When Rick moved into position, Cassie let the last few notes die away. Her senses couldn't get enough of him, his dear face and gentle smile. His voice quiet yet edged with authority, he asked the congregation to rise.

How I love him...

Cassie forced herself to look down to hide the rush of emotion that threatened to break through. This was Rick's day to show his community what his ministry was about. Today they would see how God had used him.

"He is risen," he said, his smile wide as he gazed out over the group.

"He is risen indeed," the congregation responded.

Cassie waited as he welcomed everyone. Her heart thrummed with anticipation when at last he nodded to the choir and they took their places on stage. Then Rick looked directly at her.

Spellbound by his stare, Cassie saw anxiety flicker through his green eyes. She knew he was second-guessing himself, wondering if he'd been right to encourage the kids to do this, worrying he'd asked too much.

Yes, he'd rejected her love. And come Tuesday, she would leave Churchill with her heart breaking. But today—today she was going to make sure that this man she loved with her heart, soul and mind would not regret this day. She lifted her lips in a huge smile that she hoped told him that she believed in him, that she knew today would be a success.

Faith, she mouthed at him.

Slowly, surely, his beautiful smile transformed his face. He nodded at her. *Faith.*

Then, with the choir's full attention, he lifted his hand. Cassie played the somber opening chords, thrilled as the dark low notes echoed through the sanctuary. Choir and band hit the first note in perfect unison.

Thank You, Lord.

Then Cassie threw herself into playing the music, for Rick.

Rick had arranged a Scripture reading to give the choir and band a break halfway through the Easter cantata. While they sat, John rose. Standing amidstst the congregation, his baritone voice authoritative and yet personal, he began to recite verses about that first Easter morning.

Rick got caught up in thoughts of the next part of their presentation until a pause in John's speech caught his attention. He looked up and found John staring directly at him, his dark eyes focused and intent. Then in a clear ringing tone he quoted, "'There is forgiveness of sins for all who turn to me.'"

Every cell in Rick's body homed in on that sentence. Jesus died to forgive sins, *his* sins. Hanging on to them diminished the very sacrifice he celebrated.

Light filled Rick's soul, cleansing, clarifying, chasing out the guilt and refreshing it with the joy of the Easter message. Bemused by the wonder of freedom that flowered inside, he waited until John sat, then motioned for Noah to prepare.

Forgiven. I am forgiven. His soul chanted the glad refrain.

Cassie played the entrance to the song, this time a booming, triumphant series. Rick lifted his hands and their voices responded, soaring in hallelujahs that blended and harmonized in a perfect tribute.

Then Noah's pure voice rang out, the words of redemption clear. His face shone as his solo echoed through the rafters. *Redemption. Deliverance. Freedom.*

Still lost in the wonder of the gift that took away his guilt, Rick led them to the end of their Easter cantata, every note exploding with praise for the Easter gift God had freely given.

As the last note died away, as the crowd rose and

applauded, Rick bowed with the choir, his choir, then motioned for Cassie to take a bow. In that second the truth of what others had been trying to tell him finally hit his heart. God didn't need or want his vow or his sacrifice for something He'd already wiped out. God needed a heart ready and willing to serve.

Churchill was where God wanted him.

But God had also sent Cassie here.

For him?

Hope flickered to life in a part of his heart that Rick had shut down. He needed to talk to John, to make sure his thinking wasn't off, that he wasn't making another mistake.

Can it be that You planned this, God? Love? For me?

His heart began to sing a new song—for Cassie.

Cassie snuck away from the church right after the service. She knew Noah and her father would catch a ride with Laurel. Before their Easter dinner, she needed some time to get her emotions under control, to make her heart stop hoping and yearning for something it couldn't have. By the time the boys and Laurel appeared at Lives, she thought she was in control.

Then Rick walked through the door.

Control and rational thought fled, along with her voice. Her eyes couldn't get enough of his spiky hair and his lopsided grin, and the low musical rumble of his voice. Each one seemed to resonate through her.

"Thank you for your amazing playing, Cassie," he said, his smile stretching across his face. "You made us sound great."

"That was all the boys. I just provided background noise."

There was something different about him. But though she studied him surreptitiously throughout the meal, Cassie couldn't figure out what it was. And it was hard to be so near him, to tamp down the love that burgeoned inside.

Oh, Lord, her heart wept.

So when everyone went to the family room to play games, Cassie crept away. She pulled on her coat and gloves, and left the house. Outside the sun beat down with intensity, moderating the afternoon's chill.

She was lost in her thoughts of Rick and prayers for the courage to hold fast to her decision when a hand touched her arm.

"Cassie."

Oh, that voice. She turned and rested her gaze on his beloved face, stunned by what she saw glowing in the depths of his eyes. His face shone, his voice held a depth of joy that took away her breath. "Rick?"

"I've been redeemed, Cassie." The words rang in the crisp air. He tipped back his head and laughed. "Redeemed. I don't know why I didn't see it. I'm a minister! I shouldn't have made such a stupid mistake, getting caught up in my wrong thoughts, but I did."

What was he talking about?

"God forgave me, Cassie. 'There is now no condemnation for sin,'" he recited, green eyes shining. "I've been trying to pay off a debt that wasn't there. My mistakes were all forgiven the first time I asked God. That's what Easter is all about."

"I know," she whispered, uncertain as to what this meant, and afraid to hope.

Afraid? Had she not yet learned to trust the One who loved His children enough to make the ultimate sacrifice? *I trust You. Help me, Lord.*

"Your father helped me see that my vow was wrong, that the guilt I've been clinging to is not part of His plan of forgiveness." He wrapped his arms around her and swung her in a circle, his head thrown back as he gazed into the blue sky. "I'm free!"

Startled and off balance, Cassie grabbed hold of his shoulders. Their faces were mere inches apart.

"I love you, Cassie Crockett. I love you with all my heart. Please don't go. Please stay and help me reach Churchill for God. Together we can do wonderful things for Him. We proved that today."

Inside her something released. For the first time since that awful day at his house her spirit lifted and she knew, she *knew* God was giving her the go-ahead. But just to be certain it wasn't her own will, she closed her eyes.

Are You saying yes, God?

Cassie felt Heaven's nod with every fiber of her being.

"Cassie?" Rick set her on her feet. His hand cupped her chin, his breath caressed her cheek. "What's wrong?"

"Nothing's wrong. For once everything is perfect. I love you, Rick. You're the man of my heart. I thought I'd never trust anyone again. I thought if I put my trust only in myself that I'd be safe, but God is teaching me that trust is an integral part of any relationship. I trust Him completely and that's because of you, because of what you've taught me about Him."

She had to stop, catch her breath. But she couldn't because Rick was kissing her. He started with her forehead, then her cheek, then the corner of her lips. Their breaths mingled in a cloud of vapor and then his lips met hers. He clasped her tightly to him and for a timeless moment the world stood still. Cassie reveled in the sweetness of his kisses, the rightness of being in his arms.

"I'm sorry for hurting you," he whispered. "Please forgive me."

"Of course." She rested her head on his shoulder. "I need your forgiveness, too, for misjudging you."

"Done." He sighed, pulling her closer. "Forgiveness. How is it I got so totally confused about that word? It means 'remembering no more.' And yet I kept dragging the past back, focusing on it instead of on what God has done. It took me a long time but I finally see what God's been trying to show me."

He drew back enough to see into her face. Cassie tensed with worry for a moment before she remembered that God was in charge. *I will trust Him.*

"I come with baggage, Cassie," Rick told her. "Maybe that's the wrong word, but you must know that I am dedicated to doing God's work. There's no fame, no glory and not much money."

How she loved him, loved his dedication to his Lord.

"Look around, Rick. We live in the most beautiful place in the world. Fresh, untouched, with God's handiwork all around. How could fame and glory ever compare to this?" She smiled. "Besides, you're laying up treasure in Heaven with your work. God honors that."

"So that means you'll stay in Churchill? You'll help me, share my work here?" He paused. "Will you marry me, Cassie?"

"I'd be honored to," she said. "Because I love you."

He kissed her back with heartfelt abandon. Cassie's soul sang with joy she'd once thought lost forever.

"Perhaps together we can use our mistakes to help others heal, as you've done with Noah and the boys," she murmured and pressed a kiss against his cheek. "I can never thank you enough for Noah, Rick. You reached past his angry heart and helped him begin to heal. Because of you I have my son and my dad back. And I'm building a better relationship with God."

"So am I," he said with a cheeky grin. "Isn't this a happy Easter?"

"The happiest." She turned in his arms and together they stood and admired God's handiwork. "We're going to be very happy," she said with certainty.

"I already am," Rick replied.

Epilogue

In Churchill the ice melted, the snow disappeared and the tundra bloomed as Rick's church grew, in part thanks to John's help. He'd moved to Churchill to be near his daughter and grandson, and had worked with Rick through the summer on a book for kids about getting rich with God.

In early autumn Churchill's splendor changed again to vivid red berry bushes, golden moss and bright yellow grasses. The air grew crisp, the sun blazed in the richest blue of the sky. Geese honked overhead as the land prepared for winter.

On the brightest of these days, Rick's little church teemed with activity as the boys from Lives Under Construction joined with local kids to ready themselves for the wedding of Cassie Crockett to Rick Salinger. Everything had to be perfect so they arrived well before the first guest to practice their part in the wedding.

Thus it was that when Cassie arrived at the

church with Laurel, Alicia and new-mom Sara, the band welcomed her inside. She followed her two bridesmaids down the aisle as Michael played a solo on his saxophone. Her eyes rested for a moment on Kyle, who stood tall as best man, then moved to Noah. She smiled and her son smiled back, his blue eyes twinkling. Then her gaze locked on Rick, the man who filled her world and her heart.

Her father led them in their vows to each other.

"I love you, Cassie. I love the promise I see in you, the heart you lavish on those in need, the joy you bring to my days. I look forward to our future because I know God has great plans for us. I'll be by your side always as we place our faith and our trust in Him." His gaze holding hers, Rick slid the wide gold band onto her finger, then kissed it in place.

Cassie smiled through a gloss of tears, her heart lifting. God had brought her so far.

"I love you, Rick. I love your joy in people. I love your God-centered life and your dedication to do His will. I love you for loving me, for moving beyond the past to embrace our future. I will love you until eternity." She smiled into his eyes as she slid a matching circle of gold onto his ring finger.

"As much as these two have pledged their love to each other, by the power of God I declare Rick and Cassie to be husband and wife." John grinned at them. "You may kiss your bride."

A hush fell inside the little church as Rick and

Cassie kissed. Then Noah's voice rose in a joyful a cappella solo giving praise to God for His gifts of love. Cassie's heart almost burst with pride.

What a long way they'd come. All of them.

"Ladies and gentlemen, may I present Mr. and Mrs. Rick Salinger."

Her arm looped in her husband's, Cassie took her first steps as Rick's wife while the band played the Hallelujah Chorus.

"They aren't perfect," Rick murmured in her ear as they made their way down the aisle to stand in the receiving line outside.

"None of us are. But love covers mistakes, don't you think?" Cassie shared her husband's smile.

"Love and forgiveness," he agreed.

Love and forgiveness. The two could change the world. That was the message Cassie and Rick would share with Churchill for as long as God wanted them here.

* * * * *

Dear Reader,

I hope you've enjoyed this second book in my Northern Lights series. Cassie and Rick each came to Churchill with heart problems that only God could repair. Each needed to find forgiveness but in different ways. Stay tuned for Alicia Featherstone's story in *North Country Mom,* coming in May.

In the meantime, here are my wishes for you. May you know that all your experiences are a gift, even when they aren't pleasant. May you not burden yourself by needing to find a reason for everything. May you live each moment of your day, free of worry about the future and regret about the past. And may you know the rich, abiding, uncompromising love of God that refuses to let go no matter how far we stray.

Blessings,

Lois
Richer

Questions for Discussion

1. Cassie married very young to get away from her father's neglect and hopefully find the love she craved. Do you know someone who's done the same thing and regretted it? Or someone who stayed in a bad situation and regretted it?

2. How could Cassie have dealt with her situation after Eric's death differently without becoming defensive? Should she have done things differently? Why or why not?

3. Rick got stuck on mistakes he made in the past that seriously affected his faith. Discuss ways we all struggle with accepting forgiveness and the issues that sometimes keep us trapped in our guilt.

4. Noah's bitterness stemmed from feelings of abandonment after his father died. Think of ways that people can be more inclusive to kids whose parents are going through separation, divorce or other troubling issues that often divide families.

5. Cassie felt very strongly that she needed to improve her financial situation and build a cushion. This meant she took on a lot of extra

work. Talk about stages in your own life when you had to balance your family's need for more income with the time you spent away from them. Is there a way for us to balance these needs?

6. Rick took great pride in ministering to his community and pushed himself to meet their needs. Suggest ways a church family can minister to their pastor to help him avoid getting overtaxed and make sure he has quality time with those he loves.

7. The boys at Lives Under Construction came from homes where they often felt insecure. Think of troubled kids in your church or community. Discuss ways you could help them before their problems turn into legal issues that send them to jail. How do you feel about ministering to them?

8. During his years on the street, Rick dreamed of a family of his own and love. Do you have a dream you long for and are working toward?

9. Cassie gave up her hard-won nest egg to buy back Rick's guitar. Discuss sacrifices you would make to help someone you felt was gifted increase their ministry.

10. Lucy Clow is a senior, retired missionary and has arthritis. Yet she serves as part-time church secretary, sometime pianist and general internet scout for items the Lives' boys, the church and the Vacation Bible School program needed. Is there ever a time when Christian service is finished?

11. Discuss the challenges you see in living in a remote community like Churchill. Then discuss the benefits.

12. Trust was Cassie's biggest issue. Are there ways in which you fail to trust God in your own life? Explain.